Who?

Patrick Haylock is a globally unrecognised writer who, if you discount a school sweet pea growing competition, has won no awards whatsoever!

He was born in Enfield at a very dark time in the world. It was 1:45 am, to be precise, and it wasn't too long before it dawned on him.

To make something of himself he was going to need two things – the ability to tell the difference between a green onion and a scallion, and a good education.

Wormley Primary and Baas Hill Comprehensive schools did their best to fulfil both requirements, and after giving them 12 years of his life, they gave him seven printed sheets of paper, and the knowledge that there was no difference between a green onion and a scallion.

He also learned that the difference between onions and bagpipes was that no one ever cries when you chop up bagpipes.

The certificated wisdom secured a national newspaper messenger's job, which led to an editorial trainee position, followed by a production editor's post, and progression into freelance journalism.

'Knowing his onions' helped him to successfully establish his own publishing company, design studio, online retro webstore and high street art gallery.

Patrick lives with his wife in a converted Old Essex Brewery, where he claims a 6% ABV air quality inspired him to craft this nutty *tale*.

Although a 'new voice', in the literary world, those 'in the know' will willingly testify that his gift for imaginative storytelling is engaging, and, amusingly unique!

Follow Patrick's alter ego on twitter Patthequipper@twitter.com

For...

My wife, Biffo. Thank you for inspiring me to complete this book with love, laughter, and your size six motivation. I am truly fortunate to have such a beautiful woman in my life.

I also dedicate this book to Annie, who lit the blue touch paper, my parents, brother, and all my wonderful family, particularly three special girls, Midge, Rolo, and Bing. You're all more precious to me than you'll ever know. Also, for Dave, for being…… Dave!

Patrick Haylock

PLUTO'S IN URANUS!

*Best wishes
and Kushti Bok!*

Patrick Haylock.

AUSTIN MACAULEY PUBLISHERS™

LONDON • CAMBRIDGE • NEW YORK • SHARJAH

A CIP catalogue record for this title is available from the British Library.

ISBN 9781528974165 (Paperback)
ISBN 9781528974189 (ePub e-book)

www.austinmacauley.com

First Published (2020)
Austin Macauley Publishers Ltd
25 Canada Square
Canary Wharf
London
E14 5LQ

Prefix

HAVING BEEN BORN on December 25th made Dave a Capricorn, and as a Christmas day baby he felt rare, special, and part of a very exclusive club.

But as he only ever received cards and presents on one day of the year, it also made him feel hard done by.

Another irritation of being born on this day, according to Dave, was its culpability for his obsessive-compulsive interest in cosmology and astrology.

His mother recalls that even as a young child his favourite bedtime book was *Old Moore's Almanack.*

After reading thousands of prophecies over the years, the fact that none had ever resulted in any positive outcomes did little to tarnish their validity or dissuade him from still being a believer!

However, things are about to happen that will test this resolve!

Uranus, the planet of change, and Pluto, the planet of revolution, are in historical alignment, signifying an imminent period of major toil and trouble.

When **Pluto is in Uranus**, Capricorns are in for a bumpy ride, as Dave is about to discover.

His fated decision-making will result in extraordinary, hilarious, and ominous consequences.

Chapter 1

BC (Before Calamity)

APART FROM WISHING to own a BMW, have a great adventure and to feature in a book ending with the word pancake, you could say that Dave's goals in life were mediocre but achievable.

Up to now his life had been stagnating, as were his attempts to fulfil his aspirations.

Every day always began the same: an alarm call, a nature call, a shower, and a shave.

He would skip breakfast, dash to the newsagent's, run after the bus, sprint for the train, then crawl to his boss for late arrival – yet again!

His habitual lateness was due to **OCF** – *Obsessive-Compulsive Fatalism* – which he attributed to being born on December 25th.

This syndrome made it imperative for him to read his online horoscope prior to leaving home every day.

After many years of failed predictions, today's were going to prove the spectacular exception, because **Pluto was in Uranus!!**

Even his computer seemed to be in a more optimistic mode, as, far quicker than usual, it launched Dave's horoscopic homepage.

The colours seemed more vibrant, and the information was clear, precise, and positive... and today, without doubt, it was addressing him personally.

Capricorn

'Pluto has moved into Uranus, indicating revolution, a time of rebirth, new thinking, and the sweeping out of old ways.

The risk-averse should abandon their fears and take a leap of faith, as an uncharacteristic decision will turn out well!

Those with names that contain an E D A or V should be extra vigilant, as many surprising, and unexpected, opportunities are about to come your way.

Acting upon these fortuitous omens will secure outcomes and rewards beyond your wildest dreams.

New friendships are on the horizon, and a black cat crossing your path will signify an imminent boost to your finances.

The time to be bold is Now, let impulse take the lead, because, today, EVERYTHING is coming up roses!'

He left his home very much enthused.

Striding at a brisk pace, it was not long before he came to the alleyway that he used as a shortcut to the newsagent's.

On turning the corner, he was startled by a whooshing sound and the sight of a mysterious fiery object speeding towards him.

Instinctively he contorted his body and raised an arm to protect his face. His involuntary reaction deflected the threatening object and prevented it from causing serious injury.

The object thudded into the wall and tumbled down onto the pathway.

With a hiss and a finale of sparks, it spun, spat, and then ceased to be, its fiery ferociousness expired.

His quick reactions had not only avoided harm but had also

provided him with the opportunity to identify the aggressive assailant.

Along the side of the charred yellow tube, distinctive branding revealed that it was a BLACK CAT rocket.

The auspicious event was obviously fated, and it reinforced the fact that, as predicted, a black cat had indeed just crossed his path.

Kicking the pyrotechnic to one side, he continued onto and into the newsagents.

Buoyed by the fated incident, he decided that along with his usual redtop newspaper he would buy six scratch cards and six lottery tickets.

After stuffing his change and tickets into his Thunderbirds wallet, he rolled his tabloid into a paper baton and scooted off towards the station.

On entering the platform, years of commuting served him well. He knew exactly where to position himself so that he would be in line with the doors and at the front of the queue for boarding.

This advantageous knowledge had always enabled him to corkscrew his way into an unoccupied seat.

As usual, the carriages were crowded like beehives, and after yet another uncomfortable journey, the final stop was looming.

Prior to arrival, Dave always stood up from his seat and put his jacket on. He would brush his hands along his sleeves and trouser legs to remove the creases.

After a final check of his belongings and his pockets, he would stand, waiting to leave the carriage.

Fellow travellers started doing likewise, and their jostling and manoeuvring for exit positions audibly disrupted the previously hushed journey.

Like most mornings, the train juddered to an inexplicable halt outside of the station and caused the hubbub to simmer down.

Weary passengers anxiously scrutinized each other, expressing visible annoyance at the regular delay.

Then, just as suddenly as it had stopped, the train juddered again and began to move into the station.

Once it had glided the full length of the platform and come to a halt, the chaos resumed, and the hiss of the pneumatic doors signalled the start of a manic foot race to the exiting ticket gates.

Dave could never see the merits of participating in this melee, so he generally held back until things calmed down.

Also, having been brought up not to litter, discarding his newspaper onto the floor was another practice that he avoided doing.

He would always fold his paper and place it neatly onto a seat.

But even leaving his litter in such a well-ordered manner still made him feel uncomfortable and he would have to glance around the carriage to see if there was anyone critically judging his actions.

Today, whilst peering around, apart from familiar faces, he noticed a twinkle of light glinting from the fold of the seat opposite, and as the aisle cleared, he shuffled closer to take a better look.

He could see the edge of the reflecting object, and he leaned forward and with the use of his index finger and thumb he attempted to retrieve the mystery item.

Unfortunately, he only succeeded in pushing it deeper into the fold.

Not to be beaten, he pulled at the fold and then with determined use of his index and middle finger he managed to locate the object.

After a couple of attempts he got enough purchase to remove the item and after placing it onto the palm of his hand he could now see that it was a shiny silver coin.

One side depicted the Queen's head and when he turned it

over, he discovered something quite surprising: the embossed image of a cat!

Closer scrutiny revealed that it was a 1970 Isle of Man Crown.

It may not have been black, but once again the mystical 'gods' were attempting to tell him something.

He removed his wallet from his jacket pocket, slipped the silver coin into the change section, and after shoving it back into his pocket, he left the carriage.

On arrival at the company post room where he worked, a colleague greeted him and with a knowing smirk, and an enigmatic palm-rubbing gesture.

This was in acknowledgement that it was Furlong Friday, an event that occurred on the last Friday of each month.

Being the newest member of staff, Dave was the assigned collector and guardian of the post room's monthly gaming pot.

On Furlong Friday Dave's role would also entail spending the afternoon in the bookmakers staking the syndicate's pre-agreed wagers, and, as a non-smoker, he considered that getting paid for an afternoon skive in the bookies balanced his colleague's 'Nico-time' payments on smoking breaks.

It was also custom that after the last race was run, win, or lose, they'd have a booze, and he would meet his colleagues in the 'Wobblers' where they would drown their sorrows or toast their winnings.

The Wobblers was the nickname of their regular 'watering hole' which, contrary to belief, was not affectionately dubbed because of any saucy barmaid's attire or the effects of strong alcohol, but because it was bizarrely named 'The Two Blancmanges'.

As lunchtime approached, in a routinely superstitious manner, Dave would tidy his desk before opening the drawer and remove the petty cash box. He would place it on top of the desk, unlock it, and then remove the stake money.

However, today, after opening the red metal box, the black plastic envelope that contained the tote funds revealed another significant omen. The word 'KITTY' had been scrawled onto it in Tippex, indicating more good fortune!

He left work with increased heady anticipation.

The vigorous spring in his step resulted in arrival at the bookies earlier than planned, so he decided to grab a coffee and the *Racing Post*.

After fidgeting into a tall swivel stool, he took a sip of his coffee and opened the paper to read the professional analysis of their selections.

While he scrutinised the paper, a wall-mounted speaker relaying trackside events broadcast some ear-grabbing information, and he listened intently as the airwaves crackled with breaking news.

The trackside reporter excitedly confirmed that after an administrative error, Black Kitty, the two-year-old black filly owned and trained by Iliana Plutonakis, would now be in the starting line-up for the first race at Newmarket.

He repeated, "Black Kitty IS back on the racecard and WILL be running in the first race here at Newmarket."

After the announcement, the chatterer at the trackside continued whilst the counter staff busily attended to initiating the odds for the late entrant.

With the words still reverberating in his ears, Dave looked up at the banks of screens on the wall and watched the Newmarket parade ring begin to fill with horses.

However, the images being broadcast did not correlate with either his mind or vision, and all he saw was a scene emulating a surreal Dennis Potter moment.

In his eyes, the assembled jockeys had each raised a fanfare trumpet to their lips and began to herald the fact that, today, ***Pluto REALLY was in Uranus!***

It also confirmed that Dave's day of destiny was about to begin.

Chapter 2

Kerrrrrrrrrrrrrrrrrrrching!!

ENERGISED BY THE trackside news and emboldened by that morning's Horoscopic prophecy, Dave made the momentous decision to ignore his syndicate's agreed betting choices and to follow the psychic advice.

As instructed, he was going to be bold and act upon his own initiative.

So, he decided to place the syndicate's entire ante onto 'Black Kitty'.

Which, due to late entry, was also at considerably lengthened odds.

This was it!

Things would never be the same again!

One race, one big win... double kerching!

He removed the crumpled collection of notes from the lucky envelope tucked inside his pocket, walked to the counter, and wagered the entire amount on Black Kitty – **TO WIN**.

As he lingered awaiting the printed slip, he noticed that he was alone in his selection and the counter was bereft of any other punters clambering to place the same bet.

But in the knowledge that fate wasn't guiding them, as it was him, it was going to be their loss!

The horses were loaded into the stalls and a few seconds later the starter released the lock, and... they were off, the bet and the race were both well and truly on.

Dave watched nervously as stride by stride all the horses thundered off with Black Kitty storming way ahead of the pack.

As the race unfurled, Dave's eyeballs grew larger, and he stared insanely at the bank of monitors relaying the race.

He watched with some trepidation as Black Kitty after being some lengths ahead began to lose ground to the pursuing group of thoroughbred speedsters.

Led by Fourth Dimension (the syndicate's original selection), they all quickly, very quickly, began to reel Black Kitty in, and as in all bad dreams, her legs became totally inoperable, making her incapable of staving off the determined chasers.

With unwavering ease ALL the other horses caught and roared past her.

Dave watched haplessly as Black Kitty transformed from Pegasus to pantomime horse.

Fourth Dimension, the horse he should have backed, raced ahead, and won by a comfortable two and three-quarter lengths.

What followed conspired to make matters worse – much worse – as race by race and one by one each of the syndicate's other selections each romped home in first place.

Had he followed team orders, Dave would have now been holding onto slips of paper worth ten grand.

Instead he was left clutching hold of a 'stately' or the deeds to Bugger Hall, names coined by bookmakers to indicate the non-value of a heavy loss betting slip.

Dave's gamble had also confirmed that a betting SLIP was very appropriately named!

After a ponderous amount of time, Dave managed to summon the energy to extrude himself from his seat and the betting shop.

Blinking into the bright light of reality, he stuffed his hand into his jacket pocket and fumbled out a handful of loose coins, which by his reckoning amounted to about a tenner.

He retrieved the black envelope and slid the cash down his hand and into it; he took a disdainful look at the word KITTY and then tucked it into his lapel pocket.

By following the sage advice of his online oracle, it was a mere £9990 short of what the winnings would have been.

No wonder it's called a bleeding horoscope, he thought.

Guilt and panic racked his body and the only way to relieve the burden was to go to the Wobblers and 'fess up.

After all, what's the…

God, there were far, far, too many permutations for him to even contemplate finishing that sentence!

So, he didn't!

As he set off towards the pub, his legs were working on a par with Black Kitty's, and he didn't seem to be covering very much ground.

Fortunately, his mind was operating at a much brisker pace and after a short distance a brilliant 'get out of jail' thought entered his head.

Perhaps he could lie and say that he was mugged on the way back to the pub and that the winnings had been stolen.

Not bad, he thought, but to make it truly believable he would need to report it to the police, and if he could produce a witness then case closed!

With hawk-like observation he scanned the horizon and noticed an old lady waiting at a bus stop.

Not only was she stood alone but she was holding a white stick. Bonus, a short-sighted elderly witness, the gods were smiling again.

I wonder if her name's Kitty, he mused.

He also noted that just prior to the bus stop there was a passageway in which there were some large industrial dustbins: perfect!

In an effort to remain inconspicuous, he surreptitiously made his way towards, and edged into, the passageway.

Once there, he removed one of the large bin lids and standing in the shadows he used it to clatter the walls and batter himself.

He crashed about, yelling… "THIEF!"

After a few moments, he emerged from the alleyway in a dishevelled state and he made his way towards the old lady standing at the bus stop.

Phase two of his master plan was about to be initiated.

"Excuse me, love, did you see ……"

Before he could complete the sentence and initiate the mugging scenario, the old woman interjected.

"All I saw was you roughing yourself up with a ruddy big dustbin lid. You're either a bleeding nutter or a pervert and if you don't give me some money, I'll scream, and claim the latter."

Shit... Now in a panic, Dave dibbed his fingers into his top pocket and retrieved the plastic envelope of coins and tipped the contents into her outstretched claw-like hand.

She gave the money and Dave an underwhelming glance and her obvious derision was accompanied with a scathing: "IS THAT IT?"

"Your bleeding liberties have got to be worth more than a bag of shrapnel," she hissed.

Dave winkled out his wallet, retrieved the lottery tickets and the scratch cards, and he offered them to her.

Snatching them from his grasp she bullseyed a swift forceful knee into Dave's nadgers and then followed this up with a painful shin kick.

The slam dunk came with a body blow from the white-handled shopping trolley, that Dave had mistaken for a walking stick.

As his body hinged forward, he noticed that she'd dropped one of the scratch cards, and by employing an overdramatic stumble he was able to scoop up the card and conceal it in his hand.

As he stood back upright, the words, "Piss off you loser" whistled through a set of ancient false teeth.

She might look frail, but she kicks like the bleedin' Ip Man, thought Dave, as he pitifully hobbled away with both his master plan and his attire in tatters.

Arrival at the pub was sooner than he had anticipated, or even hoped, and he paused to consider his decision to man up. Accepting that it was the right thing to do, he grabbed the brass handle of the large swing door and gave it an ineffective tug. It seemed that even the door was challenging him in his judgement call.

The weight appeared to have enormously increased, making it impossible to open.

After a self-induced struggle, he managed to pull it ajar and step into a vibrant cacophony of boisterous sound.

Through squinted eyes, he peered along the crowded bar and noticed that the end section was cordoned off with a post and rope barrier.

On the counter was a galvanized tub that contained upturned and unopened champagne and beer bottles along with a hand chalked sign that read 'Winners' Enclosure'.

As if that wasn't bad enough, he caught sight of his boss 'Humph' boisterously charging around with an attractive female jockey clinging to his back.

He was sporting a pair of ears and blinkers made from beer coasters, and she was spurring him on with a crop fashioned from drinking straws.

The assembled throng had clearly been celebrating some time and they had woven themselves into a merry racing-themed tapestry.

This was obviously a celebration for the big win that wasn't.

How the hell was he going to break the bad news?

Suddenly relaying it now didn't seem to be either a sensible or very safe course of action.

Perhaps a drink or two might give him some 'Dutch' and provide a more opportune moment to share his sorry tale.

So, abandoning woe for whooooa, he vigorously joined in the partying.

Throughout the evening, Dave valiantly tried to weave his fan-hitting news into various conversations, but unfortunately, his colleagues were all too well-oiled to listen.

In fact, the only two words Dave had managed to get heard successfully were "Same again."

His pit had become a crater!

As the witching hour approached, and everyone was preparing to leave, it took just seven croaky words from Humph to fully immerse Dave into the proverbial creek.

"Settle the bill from our winnings, Dave."

The jig was up!

Like a tasered stilt-walker Dave tumbled from his bar stool and erratically and fearfully lurched towards Humph.

Putting a boomerang-shaped arm around Humph's large Crombie-clad shoulders, he confessed, "I've lossh tit all mate!"

"Whaat yuuu lost, Daaaave?" enquired a boggle-eyed floppy headed Humph.

"The moolaaaaah, the wedge, the wongaaaaaa… I've lossh tit."

Instant sobriety hit Humph and he jolted himself upright.

Dave looked up at him: Chrrrrrrrrrrrrrrist, Humph was a big man, a very, big man!

"The bloody money!" bellowed Humph. "What do you mean you've lost it?"

"Let's organise a bleedin' search party to find it…"

"No. no, no, Hummmmmmph – you don't understand. I've not actually lossht the money…" and utilising contorted fingers to create a series of illustrative slipping-through-finger patterns, he attempted to stiffen his wobbly legs to nervously state, "I didn't win it!"

"Let me telluuuuuuuu what happened," said Dave, and, in an anxious dry-mouthed light-hearted fashion, he proceeded to relay the ill-fated saga, hoping beyond all hope that amongst those listening, someone may just be drunk enough to find it funny.

No chance – the mood and the atmosphere had distinctly altered.

From being a throng of happy-go-lucky punters, they'd instantly transformed into a vengeful pitchfork-wielding rabble, each baying for blood – Dave's blood.

When Dave had finished telling his tale of the tape, Humph inhaled and once again raised his ginormous stature threateningly.

He tilted unsteadily on his heels and looking Dave squarely in the eyes he prodded a large, gherkin-sized digit right into Dave's forehead.

"Lucky black cats, I've shit 'em!" he said.

Although the statement didn't make a lot of sense, Dave wasn't about to debate the point.

Still jabbing away at Dave's head Humph continued to share his thoughts.

"I'll tell you what your stars prophesise, sunny Jim.

"They predict that for health reasons you'll be going on an unplanned, unpaid two-week journey… from which you'll return with our bleeding winnings!

"I don't give a toss how you get it, but I am willing to bet my iron fist against your crystal balls that get it you **will**."

Comforted by his attractive young female 'jockey', Humph fumbled his coat pockets to locate his wallet, winkled out his debit card, and stomped off towards the bar to settle the bill.

The die was cast… **and the next day didn't start like every other!**

Chapter 3

AD (After Disaster)

PEERING BLEARY-EYED into the bathroom mirror, Dave hoped that the events of the previous day had all been an unbelievably bad dream, but the reflection of his bruised forehead confirmed that it wasn't.

Last night Dave had been left in no doubt that to salvage his job, his skin and his friends, he had to somehow recoup the un-won winnings and he only had two weeks in which to do so.

He needed a plan!

After making a strong black coffee in a cup emblazoned with the word MUG, Dave moved from the kitchen into a cramped, messy area beneath the staircase that he liked to refer to as his study!

A laptop and printer sat on the top of a poorly constructed, flat-packed, wooden desk, which was perfectly complemented by a similarly constructed lopsided seat.

Above this was a bowed, white-laminated, wooden shelf that contained a run of some quite perilously perched books.

Sidling sideways onto the chair he placed his MUG, a 'hilarious' birthday gift from the post room lads, on top of the desk, he stretched forward, opened the laptop, and pressed the power button.

Dragging the mug back towards him he cradled it in the palm of his hand and gazed at his digital picture printed above the word MUG.

Fitting! he thought.

His gaze then tilted upwards and along the books on the shelf.

But his pattern of thought was diverted by the abrupt start-up tone and the appearance of his astrological homepage resurrecting itself from sleepy hibernation. He watched intently as the page sprang to life.

However, reminiscent of the Newmarket trumpet fiasco, all that Dave visualised was an oversized, spring-loaded, cartoon boxing glove. It had the word 'sucker' emblazoned across it and was springing out of the screen attempting to punch him full in the face.

He was so convinced of its reality that he physically flinched and bobbed out of its way.

After a few eye-blinking, refocusing squints, the screen returned to normal, but it was noticeably less warm and inviting than before.

The cyber soothsayer's once alluring attraction now seemed dull and uninviting, but given the circumstances, perhaps this was just psychological?

Possibly!

Would he ever believe or trust in fate again?

Could he?

Should he?

Dare he?

Reflecting upon his situation for a moment, he thought to himself that as the worst-case scenario HAD already happened, surely there could be no harm in peeking.

So, he clasped the mouse and with the dexterity of a champion dart player he targeted a series of cursor arrows, to unlock the secrets of today's predictions.

What followed was going to be a test of Dave's resolve.

In large bold lettering the following statement filled the screen:

Due to unforeseen circumstances Madam Patiala is unable to publish today's or future forecasts.

We apologise for any disappointment or inconvenience that this may have caused.

WHAT!

How can that be!

UNFORESEEN CIRCUMSTANCES?

Not only was that a ridiculous statement, but it was also an astrological impossibility!

How can any astrologer suffer an 'unforeseen' circumstance?

Because, if they could, then the only thing that Dave could foresee was the fact that he had been well and truly duped.

He continued uttering profanities as he maniacally typed Madam Patiala into the search engine, attempting to discover who the hell she really was.

The inclusion of the word 'madam' was guaranteed to make the results interesting, and they included information about the opera, waxworks, circus performers and many specialist services.

Leaning into the screen, he was now ultra-determined to source information about the malfunctioning clairvoyant.

He cautiously scrolled past dozens of bizarre, mind-boggling and *seemingly painful offerings*, taking great care not to linger over or inadvertently click upon anything that looked untoward.

Ironically, it was the unlucky thirteenth page of results that showed a pertinent entry:

Madam Patiala – astrological psychic www. fortunetellersrus.co.uk/patiala_online_mystic

*– born 1950 – daughter of **Hewie** and **Wilona** Jarz – touring entertainers: – Surrey-based ...*

Click – the website opened:

Madam Patiala born Fanny Jarz in 1950 Limehouse East London.

Parents Hewie and Wilona Jarz travelling performance artists.

Hewie and Wilona worked as jobbing clowns and tumblers, before creating their own acts as Beanpole the stilt walking juggler, and Madam Patala, a Gypsy fortune teller.

They performed a double act billing themselves as the '*Throwzinnies*' a slicing dicing death-defying knife throwing act.

Effing Circus family... I knew it, thought Dave. He continued reading:

After a blossoming relationship, ambition led them to leave the big top and they created an infamous risqué comedy vaudeville song and dance act.

Billed as Hew Jarz and Little Willy they soon established themselves in the East London variety theatre scene.

They settled in Limehouse and their only child Fanny Jarz was delivered in the Whitechapel Hospital in 1950.

With minimal schooling Fanny was destined to follow her parents into the entertainment business.

Adopting her mother's stage name and persona, she began telling fortunes around the London Markets.

Her big break was due to a chance meeting with philanthropic publisher Harry Lipcudd when he was passing through Covent Garden market.

A sizeable gathering engaged his curiosity and it revealed Fanny aka Madam Patala as the centre of attraction.

This was to be the first time he had seen or even been remotely aware of the existence of Madam Patala and his first impression was that she knew how to attract an audience.

Her theatrical demeanour inspired him to introduce himself, which resulted in the offer to be a regular columnist for one of his journals.

The result of a typo on her first published column, altered the spelling of her surname to Patiala.

The typesetter and sub editor who were jointly responsible for the error, both argued that it added unintentional mystique.

They also said it gave her an identity separate from that of her mother's.

Fanny recognised them as fellow members of the poppycock club, so she didn't challenge their arguments, and Madam Patala became Madam Patiala.

Throughout a long yet modest career Madam Patiala embraced most forms of media including a recent involvement with an online webcasting service.

> Unmarried Fanny Jarz shares a home with two cats in Morden, Surrey where she chooses to live a reclusive lifestyle.

Stepping back from the screen Dave felt that he had gleaned a couple of nuggets of information for further consideration.

The first was purely whimsical, as he contemplated the possibility of **Hewie** and **Wilona** introducing their daughter into their act and re-billing it **Hew Jarz, Little Willy and Tiny Fanny**.

That caused him to literally laugh out loud – and if nothing else, he'd managed to get some humour back into his life.

However, the more useful and remarkable fact was that **Madam Patiala** lived not too far away from him.

That was definitely UNFORESEEN!

But thoughts of remonstration or retribution would have to wait as the clock was ticking and there was just shy of 13 days left to get his hands on £10,000.

He minimised the search and opened his emails.

Swiftly scrolling through them, one caught his eye.

> Ref: To credit your account with the sum of 8,000,000 dollars.

Clearly a message from Cyber CON – but… you never know!

And if nothing else it's sure to be a BOAL (Bit of a Laugh)!

After checking for malevolent attachments, he opened the file.

It read:

> From the Governor's Desk at the Central Bank of Nigeria
>
> After due evaluation of your file, which was sent to us by the Nigerian Government in

conjunction with the Minystry of Finance and the NNPC, the CBN bank has been instructed to initiate the immediate release of funds totalling 8,000,000 (eight million) dollars into your personal account.

Due to stifling financial restrictions imposed in the wake of the global banking crisis we have learned that the safest and most economical way of transferring monies to your country is through partnership with trustworthy individuals.

You have been vetted and identified as such a person.

After the transfer you will be obliged to utilise 6,0000,000 dollars (six million) to procure government assets, we shall offer instruction, the remaining 2,000,000 dollars (two million) is yours to keep as payment for facilitating this service.

We understand from our findings that you have been going through toughness and that this opportunity may help you!

Warning others who have benefited from this arrangement, have been contacted by miscreants from this country in order to try and steal their funds.

Do not go through anybody but me if you truly want your fund.

For secruatery you are advised to reconfirm to us the following information:

Your full name
Age and occupation
Marital status
Your private telephone numbers
Bank details account & sort codes

After checking your file is correct we will make release of your fund.

If you do not wish this fund pass to others in hard ways.

Officially signed

'N Swartkat

Governer CBN

That didn't disappoint... in fact, apart from a few spellings and some grammatical issues, right up until the request for personal and bank details it was a tad more enterprising than others he'd received!

Envisaging the individuals who would be gullible enough to respond and willingly forward their details was just as amusing as the letter.

In fact, his shoulders jogged up and down as he recalled a tale told by his friend Heather who worked for a local estate agent.

After showing an 'uncomplicated' couple around an extremely expensive property, they told her that once the promised funds from their Nigerian business partner were transferred, they'd be making a cash offer!

Classic!

He decided to search the name 'N Swartkat.

PING – NOT AGAIN!

You must be kidding – what popped up was almost too unbelievable for words.

The search revealed that 'N **Swartkat** was an Afrikaans mystery-crime-solving BLACK CAT. Again the troublesome feline was taunting him!

Although entertaining, the correspondence was now becoming a distraction, so he decided to try a more targeted approach and typed in the phrase:

How to get money fast?

Click

Once again, a suspicious batch of web responses populated the screen.

The majority of these were dot-com sites offering questionable solutions to acquire dollars.

This made him fretful of opening a can of malwares.

So again, he carefully hovered the cursor above the listings that he felt were the least dubious, knowing full well that whichever one he was to choose, would still be playing Russian roulette with his hard drive.

Click

No klaxon, large pop-ups, screen-multiplying images or flashing messages – relief.

He read on:

"Make FAST money – guaranteed!"

In a financial fix? – Fact!

Need a Quick injection of cash? – Fact!

Pressured by timescale? – Fact!

WELL from the moment you implement any of our 12 tried and tested money generator programs the cash will start to flow – and that's a Fact!

The solution to every problem is amazingly simple, and it can be summarized in a single word – BELIEF!

By believing that you can fix a problem, you will fix a problem!

Willpower, self-belief, and desire are the greatest motivational tools known to mankind and are the fuel for empowering achievement.

IF your need or want is imperative to you, then without doubt you will succeed in moving mountains to acquire it.

So far so good, Dave thought – he continued to read:

Simplified mathematically *a predicament* would look like one of the following equations:

Dilemma – solution = Problem

Dilemma + solution – action = Problem

Dilemma + solution + action = Result

In other words, it is of no use to see a solution to your problem without putting it into action, as it will never get resolved.

To receive TWELVE assured moneymaking solutions – ACT NOW!

Activate the modest payment button and you will receive ONE EXTRA program entirely FREE OF CHARGE but HURRY this baker's dozen promotional offer is only available for a time-limited period.

In for a penny, in for £9.99, thought Dave as he sanctioned the payment.

Click

The following solutions are designed to obtain large sums of money quickly.

1. **Borrow money from a loan shark**
2. **Forge money**
3. **Sell a kidney**
4. **Sell drugs**
5. **Steal something**
6. **Get a philanthropist to invest in your cause**
7. **Enter the lottery**
8. **Hold a yard sale**
9. **Ransom something**
10. **Blackmail someone**
11. **Cyberbeg**
12. **Pawn your valuables**
13. **Sell unwanted items online or at a boot fair**

The Kwik Fix program is subject to copyright. © Kash Cowes Fiscal Management Consultancy.

They will all work!

But without action they remain just words on a page and your financial dilemma will still exist.

Bollocks, it's from the planet bleeding obvious, another tenner down the plug hole. Disappointing, but he could console himself that it was virus-free!

He also accepted that as each proposed idea could produce a cash boost, it wasn't a total scam.

Reading through the suggested ideas again he viewed numbers 6, 8, 12 and 13 as being the most realistic.

In fact, unlucky 13 may have come up trumps again as it had sparked an idea that he could immediately implement.

If worded correctly, he might be able to re-sell his unwanted Nigerian windfall in an online auction, and if nothing else recoup his £9.99 investment.

After noting the four best options, he fixed his gaze onto the tumble of books on the shelf in front of him.

Glancing along the titles, his vision halted at a book entitled *Turning Can't into Can!* This was a dog-eared textbook of classic marketing techniques essential for the sales course that he had part-studied at evening classes.

He had to admit that he was feeling like a bit of a Can't in need of a Can.

Gingerly he removed the book from the shelf and flicker-browsed it; perhaps something in here could help trigger a solution!

Inside, a sentence warning **never attack, annoy, or insult anyone who can add to your bottom line** jumped out at him.

Advice clearly ignored by Humph during last night's forehead-prodding debacle! thought Dave.

Bending back the front cover to reveal the index page, he ran his finger down the chapter titles.

Turning theory to practice...

The first golden rule...

Want V need....

Overcoming objections...

Cost breakdown analysis...

Pausing at the fifth heading, he tapped upon it with his fingertip, then tracing his nail across to the page number he opened the referenced chapter.

He speed-read the information:

> Right product wrong price... Too high too low can be fatal if...

> It is imperative that costs are calculated accurately and correctly to understand the value/return... a method known as...

> A powerful tool in the salesman's armoury is to challenge the perception of expense by breaking down the total cost into smaller units i.e. monthly weekly daily... The unit cost will seem less daunting and more affordable....

Yes, he remembered now, cost analysis was the primary key to success or failure.

He could employ this strategy and divide the money he needed to acquire by the days or even hours in which he had to obtain it.

So, dividing the £10,000 by working hours it equated to approximately £60 per hour or £720.00 a day.

It was a starting point – but using this marketing ploy only made the reality of the task seem more daunting and less achievable.

So, to avoid any more disheartening thoughts, Dave decided he would stick with having a fortnight in which to acquire **"TEN FARGING K".**

Although yelling the sum out loud, albeit unintentionally, didn't help matters, it did trigger another option… TO RUN AWAY!

Had it not been for Humph's association with a bunch of thugs who called themselves the 'Orfapaedics', this might have been a contender!

Whether Humph's bar stool tales about their unsavoury doings were true or not, he'd rather not risk being referred to them for a consultancy.

Dejectedly he moved on and shoved the book back amongst the others on the shelf.

He picked up the note that he'd made from the Kwik Kash list and restudied the four opportunities. He decided that item 13 to sell unwanted items online or at a boot fair **was** the one to pursue.

It was Sunday tomorrow and there was sure to be a local car boot sale.

After retrieving the free local newspaper from the recycling bin, his proactive approach had boosted his energy levels and he was feeling much more enthused.

Scrutinising the events listings, he noticed that the local church was holding a tabletop event not tomorrow but that very afternoon.

Perfect: '**Operation Make Good**' would begin sooner than he'd hoped.

Dialling the number given for the vicarage, he was greeted by the voice of a joyous Reverend Black.

Asking the chances of obtaining a tabletop pitch the Reverend said: "Our seams are bursting, but turn up, I'll use the Moses staff to shoehorn you in!"

The vicar's crazy theatrical reply and camp delivery made the offer sound like a line from a Carry On film.

It was very entertaining.

Agreeing to the plan, Dave ended the call and as he placed the phone onto his desk it struck him that, although tenuously, he and the prophesied colour black had again crossed paths.

But in the absence of any cat or reference to one, he dismissed the thought and set about gathering items to sell.

It had to be said that he was now feeling less of a Can't and more of a Can!

Even the costing-breakdown exercise that he'd thought of abandoning was proving useful. It was focusing his thoughts on finding sale items to raise £360.00 – half a day's **make good** requirement.

Chapter 4

Operation Make Good – Day 1

THE RICKETY BOOKSHELF was Dave's first port of call for stock. He must have loads of 'interesting' books that he could flog.

As he removed a bundle for closer inspection the rest fell like dominoes and tumbled via the desk and onto the floor.

Ignoring the mishap, he calmly removed a pencil from an upscaled baked bean pot which, if removing the lid, the label, eating the contents and washing it out counts as upscaling, then Dave had done a splendid job.

He proceeded to pick up the books that fell on the floor and began to appraise and note the saleability of his library.

Do Ants have Arseholes? – Too rude.

Fifty Shades of Oy vey – Too Jewish.

The GOD Delusion – Too Dawkins.

Out into Space – Too precious.

There was no way that he was going to part with his 'Out into Space' album, as it contained a complete set of sentimental and collectable Brooke Bond tea cards.

Not a good start, there had to be something amongst the pile that he could bear to let go and safely peddle in a church!

He gathered a quantity of American Marvel, DC, Superman, Batman and Spider-Man vintage comics which he was again reticent about selling.

However, a quick internet search revealed their worth to be in the lower pounds, so he was happy for them to be the foundation of his sales pile.

He added a batch of Star Wars magazines that had a similar retail value.

He was now on a roll, and a promising collection of academic, marketing, photography and design books were added to the stack. The subjects should bring potentially higher values.

In his hunt to gather saleable items, he left no cupboard, shelf, or container unturned.

Once the haul was safely stowed into his car, he undertook the task of adding together the individual values that he'd noted on the inside of a torn-apart section of a cornflakes box.

Studying the estimated total and deducting 25% for unsold items he realised that there was a considerable shortfall on his optimistic target.

But if he left earlier than planned, he could stop at his parents' home and relieve them of some goodies to make up the deficit.

He checked the time on his watch and even with the detour to his parents' he still had enough time to list his Nigerian offer on eBay, and having studied media and advertising at college he understood the importance of a heading, product placement and description.

All were key elements to the success or failure of any sale, especially in the online market.

He had learned how to write creatively and turn potential negatives into positives thanks to his friend Heather. She had organised a week's work experience with the ultimate prose masters, or estate agents as they preferred to be known.

The clever use of EAAs (Estate Agents Adjectives) could even make a war-torn middle eastern property seem desirable.

> *(after shelling)*
> **A fabulous opportunity to stamp your own mark –**

> *(rubble-strewn surroundings)*
> **Low maintenance gardens**

> *(looks better outside than in)*
> **Kerb appeal**

> *(has no windows or doors)*
> **Light and airy**

> *(reduced back to its framework)*
> **Original features**

Drawing upon this invaluable experience, Dave scribbled out his listing and then proceeded to open his eBay account.

He trawled through the category options.

Business office – other – possible.

Coins – virtual currency – appropriate but not really.

Everything else – item-based services – **Credit** – could be.

He decided to enter the word 'finance' into the search category, and it returned the obscure result of **books, comics, economics, and history**.

Although it might be deemed that he was vending a bit of a

fairy tale, Dave felt that **everything else – credit** was potentially his best sales portal.

He opened the auction template and input the listing that he'd just sketched out.

FREE MONEY!
Are you Stupid or Curious?

Stupid for letting the opportunity of **FREE MONEY** pass you by?
or
Curious to find out more?

For **less cost** than **a bag of crisps** you can purchase the link to resolve the dilemma.
Act now – opportunity seldom knocks twice!

Quantity 1000 items

Buy it now 0.59 each.

Auction time 28 days

Postage FREE sent via email

Dave was confident that his chosen wording was tempting and accurate enough to avoid any legal misrepresentation.

He had also pitched it at an incredibly low price to counteract any possible repercussions from disgruntled purchasers.

AND if he managed to sell a thousand that would be 500 quid in the bank!

There must be lots of risk-takers who are in 'hard ways' and willing to take a 59p punt?

With that done, Dave was out the door and on his way.

Chapter 5
Sell, Sell, Sell

TURNING THE IGNITION key of his haphazardly-laden car, the engine wheezed, spluttered and finally started. Dave drove off towards his parents Tom and Barbara's house.

These were not their real names but ones that he'd bestowed on them after his dad insisted on living off the land, like the characters in a TV comedy called *The Good Life*.

Over the years his dad had managed to transform their once beautifully landscaped floral garden into something that resembled a crater-strewn planet.

His growing prowess was just as disastrous, and his harvests would have been destined for the compost heap had Dave and his mum not surreptitiously replaced his crops with healthy produce which they bought from the supermarket.

Carrots, leeks, radishes, spuds, beetroot, onions: over the years they'd replaced the lot.

Their act of encouragement had paid dividends twice over.

The first return came via the look on his dad's face when he marched into the house clutching a couple of handfuls of HIS home-grown crop.

He would wash his crop in the kitchen sink and sing "GREENFINGER" to the James Bond 'Goldfinger' theme tune.

The second and most rewarding bonus was when he would extol the virtues of his yield being far superior to that rubbish you buy in the supermarket.

It was priceless, and it completely exonerated their nocturnal deception.

During many years of 'switching' they only came close to getting discovered once.

This occurred after his mum switched a shrivelled *courgette* for a resplendent marrow.

Mr "GREENFINGER" was so impressed by the beauty, that he declared that he would be entering it into the vegetable growing competition at their local fete and he set about registering.

Up to that point, produce-switching had deceived no one, except his dad, but his intention to exhibit not only threatened exposure of the cloak and dibber activities but it could lead to damaging repercussions for his personal integrity.

So, 'Barry Marrowlow' (as his dad named it) couldn't go to the ball, and as reported on the front page of the local paper, "due to a mysterious act of mindless and wanton vandalism," it didn't!

His father cited *'him at number 11'* as the perpetrator and announced that this was his first and last foray into the world of competitive growing.

It's better to eat what you sow.

The reminiscences made the journey seem quite brief and in what seemed only minutes he was drawing to a halt outside a wild-flowered (weedy) garden, framing a weathered (needs painting) mock Tudor property.

Dave had reached 'home'.

Clutching a bunch of flowers purchased at the petrol station, he made his way up the garden path and let himself in.

Stepping into the hallway he made a very peculiar whistle, *sswitt sswooo*, which was followed by an even stranger response of *ooooooooh, ooooooooooooooh.*

41

This method of primitive communication obviously worked as within a moment Dave's mum appeared in the passageway and greeted him with a hug and a kiss.

"Hello, luv, how's everything going?" she enquired.

"Everything's fine," said Dave, handing her the bunch of flowers. "Nothing's changed much."

However, from her expression he could see that a mother's intuition had been triggered and she sensed that he was not being entirely truthful.

She gave a wry grin and said, "Everything's déjà vu, then?"

"I think you mean 'status quo', Mum," said Dave. She wafted him a dismissive hand gesture and turned back towards the kitchen.

After a few paces she paused, turned, gripped Dave's forearm and whispered, "Dad's started baking, thanks to that Bake-Off programme.

"There's not much we can do to improve or salvage the results of this new fad I'm afraid." She winked, smiled knowingly, and then carried on walking.

As they entered the kitchen, she asked how work was and enquired after his nice boss – Rumph?

"It's Humph, Mum, Humph… He's OK!"

"You've been there a while now, luv, hasn't he given you a raise yet?"

Only last night, thought Dave, but while getting lifted off the ground by his coat lapels was technically a raise initiated by Humph, it didn't qualify as the answer that his mother may have been hoping for.

So instead he replied by saying that he was working on it.

As she rifled through the cupboards for a vase, she asked the reason for the pleasure of his company.

After crouching over his next baking sensation, Dave's dad, Harold, or Halley as Dave's mum called him, stood upright, revealing his comedy basque-and-stockings apron.

Peering over flour-coated spectacles, the dough-splattered artisan cynically professed, "He wants something!"

"Not really, I was just passing, and I thought I would pop in for a cuppa."

"That's nice of you, luv," chirped his mother, flipping the switch of the kettle.

The raised head, eyebrows and doubting face of his father indicated that he held a differing and sceptical opinion.

The probing looks lingered long enough to provoke Dave into divulging more detail.

He explained that he was on his way to a church bazaar to sell some unwanted stuff, and that he'd stopped off to see how they were, and to offer to sell some of their redundant clutter.

"Told you," said his dad, peering back down at his dog-eared recipe book.

"Oh, that's sweet of you, luv," said his mum in total naïve bliss.

She extracted a few of plastic carrier bags from the backside of 'Archie', her novelty dog recycling dispenser, and left the room declaring that she'd got a few bits that he could take.

Leaning in towards the cookbook, Dave enquired,

"What's cooking, Dad?"

"Well, your mum's got herself involved in some kind of wilderness therapy group and she's taking lessons in worm-charming, wasp-wrangling and motivational mooing up on the common."

"*That's weird*," said Dave.

"Weird, it's bloody hysterical!" replied his dad, tinkering with the creation on the table.

"No, Dad, I mean what are YOU cooking?"

"Oh, this? I'm practising my entry for the WI home baking competition.

"I've registered an entry into the contemporary themed cake category where you give a modern twist to a traditional recipe."

Dave hadn't seen him this energised by food since the 'Halley's Comet' incident, triggered by the spectacular lighting of their Christmas pudding.

It was a simple plan that involved a bottle of 70% proof Caribbean white 'holiday' rum and an indoor firework.

The result: a pair of singed eyebrows, a scorched face, and a damaged lawn.

His dad's madcap method created a fiery fruit pudding that would not extinguish and after melting the plastic table covering, he was forced to hurl it out of the window and onto the lawn.

It continued to flicker for some hours before he decided to stamp on it and snuff out the flames.

His mum filmed it all on her phone and 'Halley's Comet' became family folklore.

The kitchen door clanged against the bin as his mum bustled back into the room.

In one hand she was carrying four heavily stretched and misshapen plastic carrier bags and in the other a collection of small boxes.

Tucked under her arm was a large cuddly teddy bear.

"I've found some bits for you, luv. These are good," she excitedly exclaimed, and carefully placed the collection of boxes onto the kitchen work surface.

She let the bear slide from under her arm onto a stool and placed the bags on the floor.

Dave took hold of the large bear.

"It's an antique, luv!"

"Is it a Steiff?" he asked, looking in the ear for a label.

"I thought it was, especially after the Irish bloke down the market told me it came with a steiff brush!

Halley glanced up and said, "Silly moo!"

She ignored him and the remark and continued rummaging inside one of the bags, until she located a set of unused raffle tickets. "I thought you'd get more money for Big Ted if you raffle him!"

Nice one, Moooover, thought Dave, mimicking his dad by mentally lampooning her new pastime.

Oblivious to his thoughts, his mum transferred her focus from Big Ted to the collection of colourful boxes, and she very carefully opened one of them.

"These are some of the perfumes that I 'acquired' when I worked at the Bring and Barter Store."

"But they're old and must have evaporated by now," said Dave.

"Perfumes don't get old, luv, they mature and become classics!" She laughed. "Look, this one's pretty much full." A fact she demonstrated by holding it to the light to show Dave the contents.

The same was true with the next two boxes.

However, the last item, a small, fabric, spring-loaded case, contained a tiny bottle of 1970s perfume called Bal À Versailles. An internet search revealed it to be a collectable rarity, worth over £100.00.

A further search also showed that the other three vintage perfumes had a combined price of £200.00.

"Wow, there's a few bobs' worth here," said Dave, placing them carefully into another bag that his mum had deftly extracted from 'Archie's' bum. "I'll give YOU the money for these if they sell!"

"Oh, that's alright, luv. You keep it, we don't need it – do we, Halley?"

She glanced at Halley who had coated himself with so much cake mix that he was gradually transforming into the gingerbread man.

He peered up at Dave and with another meaningful glance confirmed that they didn't, because their surname was Rothschild!

Dave ignored the sarcasm and told his mum that if the perfumes sold, they could argue about the money.

This left him a nice get-out clause to keep it.

Finishing his tea, he gathered the bags, gave his dad a bicep punch, his mum a hug and then left.

As he jammed the bounty into the car, his mum, who'd followed him up the path, said that she'd packed a 'little surprise' in one of the bags. She blew a kiss and let out a gentle moo.

Dave told himself not to ask and got into the car.

Chapter 6

With Odd On Your Side....

ARRIVING AT THE church, a banner advertising 'The Church Bazaar' indicated that he was in the right place.

The allocated car parking area was quite full and there was a throng of excited people gathering by the large oak doors eagerly awaiting the grand opening.

A sizeable, jovial fellow purposefully strode over towards him and from his garb it was obvious that he was the vicar.

Leaning into the car he bid a hearty hello launching straight into:

"Pitch or purchase?"

"Pitch," said Dave. "I called you earlier today and you said to turn up, and you would shoehorn me in!"

That sounded so wrong.

"Ah yes, I've found you a spot next to my thumping great organ," said the chuckling cleric.

The vicar's *double-entendre* comment was so hilarious that Dave couldn't bring himself to speak, so he just raised his thumb.

To indicate where Dave should park his car, the vicar took a few steps back and began swinging his cape-clad arms like a sailor sending flagged semaphore signals.

In a flamboyant, confident 'pulpit' voice, he issued the

instruction to go forth, and to slot her into a gap between the two buttresses at the rear.

The vicar then disappeared, but his innuendo-laden conversation left Dave with a yearning to hear one of his sermons.

Dave then proceeded, as instructed, to drive around to the back of the church.

Spotting the designated space, he backed into it and as he did a small arched-shaped wooden door opened and the vicar reappeared.

He walked over to Dave's car and hovered while Dave unbuckled and got out.

Holding out a hand the size of a bunch of bananas, the vicar pronounced himself to be the Reverend Roger Black!

I'm in a bleeding Cluedo game, thought Dave, concerned that he might be inadvertently smirking.

He gripped the large open hand and responded, "David Roberts!"

"David or Dave?" enquired the vicar.

"Dave's fine, reverend."

"OK, Dave, let's get to it – I'll show you your pitch, follow me."

He turned and briskly re-entered the church through the little doorway.

Following close behind, Dave was quite surprised to see a large contingent of stallholders, all busying themselves in preparation of the grand opening.

Coming to an empty trestle table beside a truly mighty organ, the reverend Black pointed at it and said, "There it is. She's all yours, load her up and get peddling."

"Are there any rules I need to observe?" asked Dave.

"Just one rule, when you hear the Hallelujah chorus that will be our way of letting you know that the bazaar is closed, and you must pack up and leave.

"My wife will visit you later to collect the fee for your stall, which reminds me, there are portaloos outside.

"Well I must dash; I've got to give the old boiler a stoke. If I don't, we'll all perish from the cold."

He turned and floated off.

He must do it on purpose, thought Dave as he made his way back to his car to begin unloading.

After several trips and stallholder-acknowledgement nods, his pitch was set up and even if he said so himself it looked inviting.

After repositioning a few items on the table he was ready, just in time to hear the large metal bolt on the main door clunk open and a wall of sound filter into the church.

He had decided to hold back the perfumes because even with his limited knowledge of boot fairs, he knew that the first wave of punters would be fellow 'traders', whose sole aim would be to acquire your best stuff at 'dealers' prices, and then sell them for considerably more from their pitch.

He needed the profit more than they did!

As he carefully stowed the perfumes beneath the trestle table, he realised that he'd forgotten to bring anything with him to sit on.

Looking around he observed the edge of some chairs stacked in a side room across the aisle.

Turning to his plant-selling neighbour who'd introduced himself as Foggy, he asked him if he would keep an eye on the stall while he retrieved a chair.

Apart from his name, Foggy's appearance also reflected that he was from a generation of chilled, non-conforming souls.

The array of herbs and aromas drifting from his table strengthened this supposition.

Moving quickly across the stone floor, Dave entered the side room where he had spotted the chairs.

He discovered that the side annexe was used for Sunday school and after closer inspection he realised that the chairs were designed for little people.

By now a vigorous swish of people were circulating around

the room and not wishing to miss out on a sale, he removed a chair from the top of the stack and made his way back to his table.

Thanking Foggy for keeping cave, he plonked the chair onto the floor and sat on it. However, due to its diminished size, only his head was visible above the tabletop.

At this level he could better view the vegetation on Foggy's table, and he was now sure that it was weed.

He asked Foggy if it was what he thought it was.

"And in a church! Who'd expect it?" said Foggy with a mischievous grin.

This could be an interesting afternoon, thought Dave.

It was not long before Dave's first potential sale seemed to be in the offing.

A geeky-looking individual thumbed through the pile of comics, then looked at Dave and asked if his mother or father were around.

Raising himself out of the chair and up to his full height Dave now towered above the embarrassed would-be purchaser.

"Oh sorry, I thought…"

"It's OK," said Dave. "What can I do you for?"

"I'm interested in buying these Star Wars magazines; how much are they?"

I guessed you might, thought Dave cynically.

"I'll just check." He lifted the carrier bag from the floor to retrieve and refer to his cornflake pricing chart.

Turning the cardboard cornflake packet around several times, he made a joke that *doodle* search was nowhere near as quick as *Google*.

The humorous remark failed to register even the slightest titter of response, so he fixed his gaze back onto his chart ran his finger down the list, and said the comics were a couple of quid each.

By his reckoning, there were 15 mags in decent order and

three that were a bit worse for wear, but he'd throw them in for free.

So according to his calculations it came to thirty quid for the lot.

"That's retail, and I'm trade," came the nerdy response. "What's your best wholesale price?"

Yeah, you're Darth Trader, thought Dave.

Now he was faced with the dilemma of haggling or holding firm on his price, which was a quandary that he pondered for a moment.

"Why don't you make me an offer?" said Dave firmly slapping the magazines back onto the table.

"Well, I'd say a tenner for the lot is more than a fair price."

"And I'd say that twenty pounds is less than a fair price but acceptable," said an irritated Dave who was now ultra-determined to win the price war with the comic con artist!

"Twenty quid – no way! I can buy these magazines in charity shops for 50 pence each."

A voice inside Dave's head wanted to tell Jabba the nut to do one, but he thought this might dissuade other customers from visiting his stall.

So, he calmly attempted to close the sale.

"OK, you want to pay ten pounds and I want twenty let's meet in the middle and call it fifteen." He held out his hand to bring negotiations to a conclusion.

On the point of agreement his nemesis spotted and pointed to a colourful object protruding from one of the plastic carrier bags and asked if he could see it.

Dave removed it and handed it over. "It was my old school lunchbox," said Dave.

"I am not a great fan of Judge Dredd but if you toss it in with the mags, we have a deal."

By now Dave just wanted the wanker GONE, so he accepted the offer.

As the youth strolled away, Dave lowered himself back into

the chair and, drained of enthusiasm, he glanced up at Foggy, raised his eyebrows and gave a few sideways twists of his head.

This prompted the offer of an oddly shaped cigarette from Foggy's baccy tin.

"Enlightenment," said Foggy with a twinkle in his eye.

Dave politely declined the offer.

After his blood pressure returned to normal, Dave rummaged the carrier bags for the book of raffle tickets.

Perhaps the raffle might prove more successful and certainly less stressful.

However, being such a novice trader, he had forgotten to pack any materials with which to produce the raffle poster.

Asking Foggy if he would mind the stall again, he returned to the annexe.

Hunting around for materials to make a signboard, he came across some fat markers in a box. Tucked behind a large old chest was a sizeable sheet of card. He bent it in half and along with one of the fat markers, he took it back to his stall.

Foggy was serving a customer, so Dave gave a grateful nod and a thumbs up for minding the shop.

On closer inspection he noticed that the card contained an image which he'd not seen prior to folding it.

Unhinging it flat, exposed an incredibly old, now mashed up, hand-coloured engraving depicting The Last Supper.

Literally – OMG!

He swiftly snapped the two halves back together to consider his next move.

It was too damaged to rectify or return, so the only option was to continue making the sign and to smuggle it out at the end of the sale.

He dexterously created a three-dimensional upturned 'V' which not only made it freestanding, but it also concealed the ruined image.

Then using the marker, he spelled out his sales pitch in large bold lettering:

WIN

THIS TEDDY

£1.00

per ticket

He then finished it off by drawing a border around it with some decorative hearts and flourishes.

Quite pleased with his effort, he positioned it along with the bear onto the back corner of his stall.

The dry atmosphere inside the church was making him thirsty but unfortunately this was yet again another part of his preparation that he'd overlooked – hey ho!

The hall was buzzing, and it didn't take long before another customer was stood in front of his stall.

His mental plea that the next sale might be concluded without a hitch sadly, went unheard!

The attire and accent of the female indicated that she may be of Eastern European descent.

The poker-faced woman pointed to some of the more expensive *objets d'art* on the tabletop.

Dave collected each one in turn and stood them all together.

When she had finished pointing, the woman in an abrupt manner requested the "bestest price?"

After discounting the total cost, Dave replied, "Fifty pounds."

The woman smiled and twisted both hands over to reveal her palms. In Dave's mind this meant one of three things: either that she would take them, it was too much, or she didn't understand.

As no money was forthcoming Dave decided to go with his third hunch and he responded by gesturing 'fifty pounds' by opening both hands five times.

The woman responded by opening both hands once indicating ten.

Due to the earlier 'fantastic one' incident, Dave completely lost the plot and he made a two-fingered gesture at the woman to indicate that she should go away.

However, the consequence of this action was that the woman dropped two-pound coins onto the table, gathered the items and quickly disappeared into the milling throng.

Dave spun on his heels and with two clenched fists pummelled his own head.

He looked at Foggy who once again offered up the baccy tin.

God, when was he going to attract some decent customers?

For the next hour, his heavenly appeal seemed to have been approved as he sold a substantial number of items and raffle tickets without any hassle.

The next prospect to appear before him was a small girl who approached the stall.

"Hello," he said, "how are you?"

"Fine," she replied.

"Would you like to win Big Teddy?" he said, in a shameless pitch to sell her some raffle tickets.

"Yes," she replied, "but I have to show him to my mummy first. When she sees how cute he is she'll give me some money to buy tickets."

"Where is your mum?" asked Dave suspiciously.

"She's over there in the wheelchair by the door. She can't get over here because it's too crowded.

"If I can take him to show her, I'll come straight back with the money."

Dave stretched up on tiptoe and caught sight of a woman sitting in a wheelchair by the door; he gave an acknowledging wave and she waved back.

"That's OK," he said, and he handed Big Ted to the little girl who meandered her way towards the woman.

He anxiously watched as Big Ted's ears threaded their way back and forth through the crowd and finally stopped beside the wheelchair. On arrival, the woman sitting in the chair took hold of the bear, stood up, waved at Dave and then she and her mini-accomplice both ran out of the door.

"BOLLOCKS!" yelled Dave, which momentarily hushed the assembled throng.

This time he took a ciggy from Foggy's tin and went outside.

Putting the reefer between his lips he realised that he'd failed yet again – he had no matches.

Just as well, he thought, and he began to take imaginary drags on the cigarette which strangely enough produced a relaxing effect.

After about five minutes he re-entered the hall to return to his stall.

On the way, he spotted a teddy bear for sale on another stall. He decided to buy it and salvage his raffle.

Even though it was knitted, stripy pink and quite a bit smaller than the original, who was going to notice?

Although not the perfect solution, it was a better option than having to make refunds.

Arriving back at his stall he gave Foggy his ciggy back and then glanced at the time on his phone. He hadn't realised just how fast it went when you're having so much fun!

The time had come to unpack the perfumes and arrange them for sale, and after creating a nifty display, he sat back down into his pixie seat and grabbed the carrier bags to look for his mum's 'surprise item'.

After a few minutes of unsuccessful exploration, an extremely sweet smell permeated his nostrils, which he assumed was wafting from Foggy's herbal emporium.

However, after glancing over in Foggy's direction it was clear that he was in smoke-free mode, so where was the delightful smell emanating from?

Diverting his eyes to look to the front of his table, he found the answer: it was drifting from a muscular female sporting what looked like a five o'clock shadow.

She was studying the perfumes and seemed particularly interested in the Jean Desprez Bal À Versailles.

"Are these all original?" she asked in a gruff voice.

"Yes," said Dave, trying hard not to stare. "They all belonged to my mother and she tells me that the one you're holding is a 1970s un-tweaked original formula, not to be confused with the later 1980s release.

"It meant something to her," he said in defence of his knowledge.

"Well, they've got my name on them, how much for all four of them?"

To demonstrate sincerity, Dave now made direct eye contact with the character standing before him and it became obvious that the femme fatale was clearly someone who enjoyed a walk on the wild side!

"I checked them out and they're worth about £300.

"But, for all of them.... **two hundred?**"

Expecting a counteroffer Dave was surprised by the response.

"I don't have the cash on me, but if you're willing to take a deposit, they're sold!"

A white gloved hand reached across the table to seal the deal. No haggling, at last… Karrrrboom!

Dave leaned forward and eagerly shook hands and he was amazed at the crushing pressure being exerted through the dainty glove.

Rifling into her expensive clutch bag, the woman withdrew and handed over a crisp **£50.00** note.

"If you could drop them round to me later, I'll have the rest of the cash, and I'll add another tenner for your trouble."

She searched into her bag again and handed over a printed card.

"I'm Jo, I live just around the corner."

Dave responded by saying "Dave," and they shook hands for a second time.

Deal done, she moved over to Foggy's table where she paused long enough to gather a small leather pouch. She discreetly slipped it into her handbag and then sashayed out of the church.

"You obviously know her?" said Dave, not wishing to pry too deeply.

"Yeah, everyone knows Jo-Joe! He's Joe with an E when he dresses as a man, and Jo without when he doesn't. He owned a variety booking agency and still likes to dabble in Panto."

"I can see that," said Dave, who was now slightly troubled that he'd arranged to go to Jo's home.

However, he was less anxious after Foggy confirmed that both of Jo-Joe's personas were harmless and great fun to be around.

In the brief time that Dave had known Foggy he felt confident in trusting his judgement.

Buoyed by the sale, Dave felt the urge to tell his mum.

Calling her on the mobile he conveyed the good news.

"That's brilliant, luv, I'm really pleased for you."

"Thanks, Mum, I'll give you the money."

"Don't want it, luv, you keep it."

"We'll talk about it."

"We already have – you keep it."

Just about to end the conversation, he remembered the surprise item.

"Mum, I looked, but I couldn't seem to find the surprise item you packed, what was it?"

"It was in your old school lunchbox, luv: I put a snack, a couple of your dad's miniatures and a £20.00 note to pay for the stall."

The word "Bollocks" again inadvertently burst from Dave's

lips and just as before it echoed around the church and caused another noticeable lull in the hullabaloo.

"I hope that wasn't the vicar," said his mum.

Dave was now so annoyed with himself for getting involved in the ever-escalating disaster that was his first sale, that his mum's whimsical comment fell on deaf ears.

"Well thanks, Mum, got to go – see you later."

So, not only had he allowed himself to be shafted by Luke Scamwanker, but he'd also provided him with a Happy Meal and a free monetary gift!

"Bollockkkkkkkks."

He had to stop saying that, otherwise people would think he'd got Tourette's.

Returning to his tiny seat he managed to encourage a few more sales, making the day, after a shaky start, quite a fruitful one, which was particularly boosted by the sale of the perfumes to Jo.

He was about to check the time on his phone again when over the PA system, a powerful rendition of the Hallelujah chorus rang out.

HAL-LE-LUJAH! It was over, and up to this point the vicar's wife had not appeared to collect his stall money.

Perhaps she'd forgotten, or they were going to let him off without paying?

Either way if he was quick, he might be adding twenty quid to his bottom line, so he began by hurriedly removing and securely packing away the 'valuable' raffle sign.

He hoped that this might help avoid its exposure and having to fulfil the draw.

He was WRONG!

He noticed that there was a flustered feminine hurricane swirling a pathway through the malingering shoppers and she was heading straight towards him.

As she got closer, the woman extended her arm and clutched onto Dave's forearm with her hand.

She gathered her breath before explaining that her husband, the vicar, had only just reminded her to collect the rent from the organ chappy.

"I was worried that you might have left!"

"You needn't have worried, I wouldn't dream of leaving without paying," said Dave, hoping that God wasn't privy to his earlier thoughts.

In the absence of any lightning striking him he asked what the 'damage' was.

"Oh, there's been no damage," she said misunderstanding the vernacular. "I just need to relieve you of a £20.00 donation for the stall.

"That's fine, Mrs Black," said Dave handing her a crumpled purple note from his pocket.

"Bless you," she said. "My name's Catherine, but everyone calls me Cat."

She held out her hand which Dave shook and responded by saying, "David – Dave."

"Very pleased to meet you, Dave, and thanks for your support today. I genuinely hope we'll get to see you at another one of our fundraiser events." She then turned and left.

What a nice lady, thought Dave, pleased that he had not absconded without paying.

While packing his unsold items, he became aware of a small gathering of children congregating to the side of him.

The tiny voice of a small girl clutching a bundle of raffle tickets piped up.

"What number won the teddy, mister?"

Having been caught off guard Dave said the first high number that sprang to mind, "185, it was ticket number 185."

He hadn't a clue how many tickets he'd sold but he felt extremely confident that it was far less than 185.

So, the odds that any of the assembled horde would have the winning number, had to be stacked in his favour.

WRONG AGAIN!

Just as in the bookmaker's, 'misfortune had favoured the Dave'.

The group formed a small circle and frantically shuffled through a dubious mixture and amount of raffle tickets.

After a sequence of dextrous hand manoeuvres befitting of a 'find the lady' scammer, one of the girls turned around and excitedly yelled, "I'VE WON IT, I'VE WON!"

She ran up to Dave and thrust the ticket at him, looked back at her friends and breathlessly repeated that she'd won BIG TED!

"Well done," said Dave examining the ticket in incredulous disbelief.

He was convinced that her winning ticket was totally different in size and colour to those in his raffle book.

But as it was securely tucked in with the 'Holy' sign he wasn't going to unpack it or create a scene to contest the claim.

It was best to hand over the prize and have done with it! So, he located the replacement knitted teddy, and handed it to the lucky winner.

The little girl looked at it, instantly stopped her victory dance and screeched that it was not BIG Teddy!

She wanted BIG TEDDY!

Dave tried reassuring the girl that it was BIG-*ish* Teddy, hoping that she would take it and go away. Eventually after stamping her foot angrily and snatching the bear, she and her friends did leave by running out of the church.

"Thank you, God," said Dave – looking upwards, and he returned to packing his items.

Moments later a clatter of noise drew his attention. It was coming from the distraught little girl, her friends, and an exceptionally large and threatening-looking man who were entering the church.

When they got close enough to invade Dave's privacy, a guttural two-vowel sound emanated from the large tattooed man.

"OI! What's yer game?"

"It's a different teddy, Uncle Mike," said the little girl, loading the big fella with ammunition.

"She's right, this ain't the same Teddy Bear that was in the raffle – we want the BIG TEDDY! Not this poxy little pink knitted thing," and he proceeded to twist and shake it in front of Dave's face.

"This little girl won 'im fair n' square, so 'and 'im over."

"I'd love to do that, Mike…"

"Mr Oxlong to you," came the reply

Surely not, he's taking the piss – Mike Oxlong. That's a joke, not a name, thought Dave, desperately trying not to laugh and further inflame the situation.

Dave bit the inside of his cheeks for a moment before continuing with his explanation.

"It's like this, Mr Oxlong, I did have a bigger teddy in the raffle but …"

His explanation about the theft was curtailed when the little girl who had absconded with Big Teddy appeared and proceeded to hug the man-mountain confronting him.

You couldn't make it up!

What emerged next was even more bizarre.

It transpired that cuddly Mr Oxlong was also *her* Uncle Mike and she was relaying a message from her mother to ask if he could collect them from the chip shop.

"Of course, sweetheart," said big-hearted Uncle Mike, and he proceeded to ruffle his niece's hair with his great big hand, which was seemingly a characteristic trait within this parish.

"Tell your mum I'll be there after I've sorted out a little problem."

There are certain words you don't wish to hear from villainous types and 'sorting out' are two of them!

The girl left, and Uncle Mike's big craggy face loomed back into Dave's. "You were saying?"

Dave's endorphin-stimulated brain assessed the situation at the speed of data flowing through a fibre-optic cable.

There were three potential responses and possible outcomes to resolve the problem.

The first was to be truthful and tell Uncle Mike that his niece was a thief – outcome, not good.

The second was to stand his ground and front it out with Uncle Mike – outcome, hospital.

The third least provocative and probably safest course of action was to… lie and pay them off.

Although the outcome to this option was unknown, it was worth a try.

"The slightly larger teddy that was in the raffle, had coffee spilled over him, and I had to replace him with pink teddy. But before I was able to explain this and say that pink teddy also comes with a crispy ten-pound note, your niece had run off to find you."

"You hear that, Willow? You've won that bear and two tenners!"

"Not two…" spurted Dave, but before he could point out the miscalculation, Uncle Mike cleverly interjected by questioning if there were possibly *more* than two tenners?"

"No, it's definitely two," said Dave, accepting defeat, along with the realisation that if ignorance is bliss, then mighty Mike was deliriously happy.

So, forsaking all hope of bettering his adversary or having any further meaningful discussion, he handed over a twenty-pound note to the small girl.

To avoid any further repercussions, he clarified to her that TWO tenners make ONE twenty.

"SORTED," said Big Mike, holding out his hand.

Dave shook it and returned to packing his stock.

What an afternoon!

Chapter 7

Lord Elpus...

STEPPING THROUGH THE tiny doorway and into the car parking area, Dave saw a bilious cloud of smoke. As it dissipated it revealed Foggy leaning against his bike and foliage-laden Heath Robinson trailer.

"Bit of trouble?" he asked.

"Just a bit," said Dave.

"I thought that. I hung about in case you needed an ambulance. That bloke's a total nutter, you know?"

"You reckon?" said Dave sarcastically.

"Well I'm glad to see that you're OK," said Foggy, straddling his cycle. "I'll see you around." He then peddled off into the night.

Dave studied the address details on the card that Jo had given him and tapped them into his sat nav.

He waited for the satellite to 'lock on' and once it had, the voice of Del Boy (his celebrity choice) began to issue instructions to guide him towards the *destinashun*.

Unfortunately, Dave was in the habit of responding far too early to commands and after four left turns he'd managed to drive in a complete square and ended up back at the church.

At least he now knew there were four, close, successive left turns ahead.

Within a short distance of following the repeat instructions, he was pleasantly surprised to hear 'Del Boy' announce: "Luvvly jubbly! you've reached your *destinashun*!"

Jo wasn't lying, she really did live just around the corner.

After parking, Dave checked the address by the car's interior light.

Happy that he'd found the right house, he retrieved the perfumes from the passenger seat, made his way up the pathway towards a front door that contained a stencilled image of a Punch and Judy tent, with Mr Punch, Judy and the Crocodile eating a string of sausages.

A Banksy! WOW!

Mounted onto the wall beside the door was a sign that read, '**Bun Id Ye Ho**', beneath which another stated:

Doorbell broken
YELL OUT
DING DONG or USE THE
DOOR KNACKERS!

Attached to the door was a solid brass knocker that was undeniably shaped like pair of gonads.

The lesser of two equally embarrassing evils seemed to be the option of using the door knackers, so he lifted the gonads and smacked them firmly against the door.

Within a few moments a brawny man in a cotton sports vest opened the door.

"Oh, I'm sorry, I was looking for Jo," said Dave.

Holding out his hand, the masculine figure said, "I'm Joe, the other one's hanging in the wardrobe upstairs."

"Not literally, I hope," said Dave.

"Not literally," said Joe, inviting Dave in.

As they walked through the hallway Dave had to ask if it was a genuine Banksy sprayed onto his front door, to which Joe replied, "Am-dram set painter, love."

"Why Punch and Judy?" asked Dave, and Joe pointed to some photographs of him performing the show on Brighton beach.

"That's how I got into show business.

"Back in the day **that was a way to do it!**"

BOOOO and hiss, thought Dave.

They entered a sweet-smelling, candlelit, Moroccan themed lounge, where it transpired that the fragrant smells were not just permeating from the scented candles, but also from a dishevelled figure sitting cross-legged in the corner.

As Dave moved closer, he recognised that the figure was Foggy.

"Welcome to **Bun Id Ye Ho**," chuckled Foggy as he bumped knuckles with Dave.

"I noticed that outside," said Dave. "It sounds like a Spike Milligan Goon song?"

"It's an anagram," said Foggy. "I'll let you figure it out."

"What are you doing here?"

"The Bobo bush works in mysterious ways," said Foggy, who after a chortle began rolling a joint.

Relieving Dave of the perfumes, Joe proceeded to slide open a concealed compartment in a coffee table that had been repurposed from a rustic ancient wooden door. He removed an assortment of notes and handed Dave **£160.00** and the remainder he gave to Foggy.

The little pouch, thought Dave, and it became clear why Foggy was there.

"Foggy tells me you've had an interesting day, sounds like you could do with a beer."

"I could," said Dave, lowering himself onto a large round leather pouffe next to Foggy.

Whilst Joe fetched the drinks, Foggy lit and offered over his spliff, which this time Dave accepted.

After drawing in a lung full of smoke, he asked Foggy how he'd met Joe.

"By accident, literally.

"The alleyway behind Joe's is a shortcut to my digs. I stopped to check my phone and I leaned against his fence which collapsed and deposited me, my bike and wagon all over his garden.

"Joe offered me a drink and we discovered that we shared a common habit."

"Not dressing up?" said Dave.

"No, *this*," said Foggy, pointing at the herb.

Joe returned to the room carrying drinks and some nibbles, and after handing them around he sank into a large leather bean bag, and asked Dave how he'd ended up being at a church tabletop sale.

"I thought that sort of thing was more the domain of the WI, crafters and charitable causes – no offence, Foggy."

Over a period of several drinks, Dave relayed his sorry tale, at the conclusion of which Foggy stated that he thought he was unlucky!

Having listened intently to Dave's tale of woe, Joe said it was obvious that Dave needed help.

Getting to his feet Joe blew out a couple of the scented candles, indicating that it was time to leave.

After suggesting he call Dave a minicab, he disclosed that he was hosting an afternoon soirée tomorrow that his dear friend Lord Elpus would be attending.

"Lord E is incredibly wise and well-connected, and if anyone can help resolve your predicament, I'd bet my shirt that it would be him!

"Sorry about the analogy."

Joe insisted that they join him, so he could introduce Dave to Lord Elpus.

On arrival of the cab, Joe said that there would be a stylish blend of 'interesting' characters attending tomorrow, so they should wear their best frocks!

As Dave and Foggy walked up the pathway Foggy turned

to Dave and nervously whispered, "I haven't got a frock, have you?"

Dave said he hadn't, "But I think he means to wear our best clothes."

"I hope you're right," said Foggy.

Arriving home, Dave counted his takings, which added up to an impressive **£385.43p.**

He stashed it into the drawer of his rickety desk and called it a night.

Chapter 8

Down The Rabbit Hole...

NEXT DAY IT was Jo who was hosting the gathering and she was holding court in the 'garden room'.

When Dave entered, the gathering was effervescing in sound and motion and his presence went undetected.

Removing a glass of fizz from a waiter's tray, Dave surveyed the room, and he got the distinct impression that he'd tumbled down the mystical rabbit hole landing in as equally a strange land as Alice's.

There were so many wacky and colourfully-dressed characters in attendance that even Lewis Carroll's idiosyncratic imaginings would have struggled to craft the assembled throng.

Dave now grasped Joe's definition of 'best frocks', and he felt somewhat underdressed for the occasion.

The Reverend Black was in attendance and was talking with Jo. He too had very much entered the spirit of the gathering, and was sporting an orange bowler hat, a pastel suit, a bright shirt, and a bow tie over his dog collar.

He was unquestionably the mad hatter.

His jolly wife Cat was standing with them and she was wearing an equally ostentatious outfit that was radiating a disco ball sparkle. They both made very bold statements of eccentricity!

Dave made his way over to greet Jo and was caught off guard when she planted a greeting kiss on either side of his face.

"None of that French La Bise stuff in the clergy," said the ebullient clerical figure as he stepped forward to proffer his giant hand in greeting.

The minister's comment made Dave feel slightly ashamed that his nervous reaction to Jo's welcoming peck may have been less conspicuous than he thought.

As he reciprocated the handshake the vicar recognised Dave and enthusiastically declared, "You're the chappy that I shoehorned in yesterday."

Jo put her hand on Dave's shoulder and said, "This is Lord Elpus."

She then asked Dave if he thought that the reverend looked like a Congolese Dandy in his outfit.

The only Dandy thing that Dave was familiar with was Korky the cat in a kid's comic, and as he didn't need another black cat darkening his doorway, he simply agreed that the vicar looked 'dandy'!

Mrs Black said that she thought the flamboyant outfit really suited him and she leaned forwards to say, "Hello again," and shake Dave's hand.

As Jo was about to expand her thoughts, she was abruptly interrupted by the sound of breaking glass and a noise that resembled a fiercely struck cymbal.

It emerged that the percussive sound had been created by a serving tray coming into forceful contact with someone's head.

Well, not just someone's, it was Foggy's.

A circle had rippled outwards from the centre of the incident, revealing an ashen-faced Foggy and a young Chinese member of the catering staff.

The parquet flooring was covered in champagne, broken glass, and a badly dented serving tray.

After surveying the scene, Jo asked what happened.

Foggy apologised stating that all he'd done was to ask this young lady her name and she said *Fuck you!*

"So, I said 'Fuck you' back and somehow the drinks ended up on the floor and I got smashed over the bonce with the tray."

At this point a senior catering colleague stepped forward to speak.

"I believe there may have been some confusion here," he said, and he went on to explain that the young girl's name really was FOOK YUEH, and she was the daughter of SOOD and LOOV YUEH!

In recognition of their names, two more of the catering staff moved forward and gently bowed their heads.

Whether the explanation was true or not, the embarrassing situation was diffused, the cacophony of sound resumed, and the party continued.

After mingling amongst some of the most entertaining characters he'd ever meet, Dave was once again back in the company of Jo.

Dave said that he hadn't discussed his predicament with the vicar yet and enquired as to his whereabouts.

"Well I've got some good and bad news on that front," said a slightly inebriated Jo.

"The bad news is that Mrs Elpus has performed a reverse miracle, and she's turned far too much wine into water, so Lord E is taking her home. But the good news is, that we discussed your plight and he's sure he can help!"

At this point in the conversation the vicar returned, and he bid Jo a very theatrical adieu.

Then gripping Dave's shoulder with his sizable mitt he proclaimed, "You're going to see my melons up the pokey tomorrow."

He grinned, shook hands, and departed.

Dave looked perplexed

"That's what happens after spending five years preaching in the East End of London!" said Jo.

"Lord E's a faith-based prison mentor. He runs a rehabilitation programme teaching felons, or melons as he likes to call them, new life skills to lessen their chances of reoffending and being returned to the pokey.

"He's confident that by using some of their 'old' life skills and 'out of the box thinking', they'll be able to find a solution to help fix your dilemma.

"He suggested we convene here at noon tomorrow, and he'll take us up to the 'big house' to meet them."

Not wishing to sound ungrateful but feeling somewhat obligated to go along, Dave simply said OK and that it sounded like a plan.

"Good," said Jo, "I'll see you at twelve," and she twirled away to continue circulating the room.

After failing to find Foggy and seeing that Jo was totally engrossed in conversation, it was an opportune time to slip away from the gathering.

Using the knacker's knocker to pull the front door closed, Dave strode briskly up the path. He heard some giggling coming from the alleyway, so he peered around the corner to investigate. To his surprise the source of the merriment was originating from Foggy and Fook.

Apart from each other's company, they were also both enjoying one of Foggy's relaxing smokes.

In a gravelly smoker's chuckle, he informed Dave they'd made up, and he extended his arm outwards to offer Dave a drag of his roll-up.

"No thanks," said Dave. "I'll catch you later."

"Fine," said Foggy. "I hope things work out for you."

Chapter 9

Cell Brains!

NOT WISHING TO be late, Dave arrived at Joe's twenty minutes early.

After giving the door knacker another hefty rat-tat-tat he was relieved to find that it was Joe who opened the door, and apart from a couple of painted fingernails, he looked every inch a 'geezer'.

It had to be said that the thought of turning up to a prison with a vicar and a transvestite to meet some hardnosed lags, although it sounded like the start of a funny joke, it had filled him with trepidation.

The vicar arrived punctually at 12 noon, and he was driving a 1960s Morris Traveller.

Once they had boarded and buckled, prior to their departure the vicar opened the glove compartment and rummaged through a hoard of what appeared to be old paperbacks; they were in fact original eight-track cassette tapes.

He retrieved one of them and, like putting a slice of bread into a toaster, he slotted it into the vintage player.

Then, they were off.

The choice of music he'd selected was both amusing and illuminating, as it was Benny Hill's greatest hits.

After listening to 'The Harvest of Love', 'Gather in the

Mushrooms', 'Yakety Sax' and of course 'Ernie', it did, if nothing else, shed light upon the inspiration for the vicar's penchant for double-entendres, or as he might have said, it exposed the fountainhead!

Some distance into the journey, the car suddenly and without warning veered to the right and sped off the main road.

They were still travelling at quite a lick when a large metal barrier loomed up before them, and only a forceful right boot brought the jalopy to an abrupt halt and stopped them from being decapitated.

"I always do that," said the vicar, "one day I'll remember it's there."

"One day, you'll be chauffeuring your own head," said Joe.

The metal arm juddered skyward allowing them entry.

"ANPR," said the reverend putting his thumb up at the security camera.

After managing to park in the middle of two designated parking spaces, Reverend Black turned off the engine and fished out a tatty old bible from his door compartment.

He then proceeded to contort and extract his sizeable frame out of the car.

Both Joe and Dave managed to exit the car with considerably less effort.

"Lock the door, lads, we don't want Moira to lead any of these poor sinners into temptation.

"Then again, I think she's probably more rust-worthy than lust-worthy."

He gave a hearty laugh.

As they walked toward the visitors' entrance, he continued his conversation.

"Her tatty appearance is the main reason that I use her for this gig… that and the fact she's the only car I own!"

Again, he expelled another raucous belly-laugh.

"You know that since coming here I have learned some particularly useful motoring tips.

"I could now get into most vehicles and start them without the need of a key.

"Useful… If I ever lose my car keys, I can still make it home!

"A couple of wheelmen have told me that with a few strategic tweaks, I could turn Moira into a kick-ass speedster.

"To be honest, I like her ass just the way it is, slow and steady."

Until she heads towards a metal barrier, thought Dave.

After security checks and the obligatory pat-down, the three of them were shown into a room that had frosted, metal-barred windows and contained a row of chairs placed in a semi-circle.

There was a large easel and whiteboard beside which was a small table containing a single felt-tipped pen and a cloth.

In one corner was a water dispenser and beside it was another seat which had the word 'Kangaroo' scribbled upon it.

This didn't make a great deal of sense to Dave until a prison officer – screw – 'Kangaroo' – came in and sat on it.

After taking their seats nearest the whiteboard, the main door was unlocked and in traipsed a group of men, all varying in appearance, shade, size, and attitude.

Once settled, the vicar rose to his feet and proclaimed a hearty, "Good afternoon, gentleman. I hope that I find you all well.

"I see that we have an empty chair and that Tosh hasn't joined us today. Is all well?"

To this enquiry, one of the older and obviously more superior lags called George, aka TC (Top Cat), spoke up to fill in the detail.

"They've put him back on the brake fluids (medication). He's been getting them anxiety attacks again, cos he's now convinced himself that one of his family is trying to kill him.

"He also thinks that he's a bleedin' millionaire investor on *Dragon's Den.*

"He's potty and potless."

74

"Oh, dear I can see why HE'S OUT then!" exclaimed the reverend.

The witty comment didn't raise even the faintest titter, so swiftly moving on, he advised them that, "As Kool would say to HIS gang: 'Let's get down on it'.

"You'll have noticed that I have invited two colleagues along with me today, one of whom I am hoping we can help to get out of a tight spot."

A gruff-voiced man the size of a hippo said, "I hope it's the pretty one."

Joe blushed, in presumption that it was he who was being singled out.

This didn't go unnoticed by the large lummox who pointed at Joe and grunted, "Not you," and rededicating the gesture at Dave, he said, "Your sister."

"Ease up, Ned," said Father Black in a calm, authoritative voice.

The reverend began to relay the details of Dave's sorry predicament when he was interrupted by the sound of a door being opened and in came a rotund, jolly individual.

On entering the room, the latecomer performed a strange sideways jig, did a muscleman pose and shouted, "'Ave it!"

He then went and sat in the vacant chair.

He looked directly at Reverend Black and said, "Aftnoon lieutenant why we punchin' the clock today then?"

"Well, Tosh, it's great that you've managed to join us and we're trying help a friend who's got into a dilemma."

"I can't bear those bleedin' Tibetan gangs, they nick bibles, and bracelets then fence 'em on the street, in broad daylight, I 'ate 'em.

"Their outfits and haircuts are both shit – I'm not investing!"

George erupted in laughter, and the others felt obliged to join him.

The vicar diplomatically ignored the laughter, along with Tosh's misunderstanding of the word dilemma, and he told him that he could decide on his investment, after he'd heard all the facts.

He continued and relayed the tale of Dave's unfortunate and sorry plight.

The outcome of this was a room filled with deafening silence, probably caused by the presumption that it was always George's prerogative to speak first.

However, it wasn't George, but Tosh who broke the silence, and he roared out the words, "I'M IN.

"I will give YOU all the money you need, and," he said, pointing directly at Dave, "in return, I want you to phone all my relatives and say I'm dead.

"I want you to make a note of their reactions and then tell me how upset they each were.

"I'll then know which one of the bastards wants to kill me."

He then stood up swivelled around and started yelling.

"Where's me fucking money?

"Which one of yous 'as nicked it?

"It was right 'ere," he said, pointing to the floor.

"Stroll on, you lot are givin' me a bleedin' 'eadache, 'oo's 'ad it?

"Come on, oo' was it?"

Tosh worked himself into such a state that, the 'kangaroo' had to leave his seat and marshal him out of the room.

As he ushered Tosh out the words "I'M IN, I'M FUCKING INNNNNNN, FUCKING IN" boomed out, and echoed along the corridor until he was back in his cell.

"Told you he was Tonto," said George, referring to his earlier assessment of Tosh.

"As entertaining as that was, I do believe that what we really need are some more practical solutions. So, who wants to go first?" asked the reverend, attempting to refocus the group.

Ned slowly raised his hand to speak.

"If your idea involves anything to do with showering,

grappling, or a combination of the two, then you can lower your hand, we don't wish to hear it!"

Ned's arm wilted back down.

"Anyone else? Come on lads, think!"

George interceded again.

"I think you've credited this lot with abilities they don't possess.

"You forget that they're all in here because their lousy attempts to acquire wealth have all fucked up and backfired.

"I can't see how any of their bleedin' ideas are gonna help you!"

"They most certainly will," retorted the vicar, "because although misused, each of you has a marvellous gift for thinking creatively."

"Well fucking Tosh certainly has," said George.

The others hooted in unison.

"What about you, Banger?" asked the vicar.

"Well, as I got done for taking one frigging sausage home from work, I can't see how that can be considered particularly clever, creative… or even fair!"

With his thumb under his chin and his crooked index finger resting between his lips, the reverend reflected thoughtfully and then responded to Banger.

"I can honestly say that the theft of a fully-automated, high-capacity, stainless steel sausage-making system cannot, by any stretch of the imagination, be considered a single sausage crime.

"Even if it did contain just enough ingredients to produce a solitary sausage.

"Let's face it, Banger, it took an awful lot of planning and logistics to implement that crime.

"A lot of thinking!"

"Yeah, I was thinking alright," murmured Banger, "I was thinking that I wouldn't get bleedin' caught!"

"And you wouldn't have if you hadn't been dumb enough

77

to store it in yer poxy garage, and try to sell it to an off-duty copper down the pub," said George, in his usual superior cynical manner.

Banger was clearly annoyed by the comment and to prevent any further dispute, the reverend made light of the statement by adding… "I'm guessing that as the officer was also a vegetarian, you could say it was doubly bad luck."

He continued.

"Cell brains – gentlemen, that's what we're dealing with here.

"Cell Brains."

He tapped his index finger against the side of his temple.

"Your brains always lead you to a spell in a cell, so you've become fearful of using them."

He raucously laughed out loud.

"You must be able to provide a few workable suggestions. Think, lads, think."

The light-hearted approach worked, and the discussion began in earnest.

George excused himself from the room and after he left the others became much more enthused and animated. A peculiar range of ideas began to flow, and each was recorded onto the whiteboard.

The ideas were all definitely 'outside the box' and they included:

Killing Humph, borrowing Ali's magic prayer mat, delivering drug-laden pizzas for Dense Al's brother, holding a dead donkey raffle, taking allotment vegetables and flowers from cemeteries, and street tubs to sell at traffic lights, auctioning your forehead for advertising space, removing and selling bus shelter posters, taking spoof charity collection canisters door to door, selling pennies blessed by the Pope, removing the tops of parking meters for their contents, hypnotising Humph into forgetting the debt and an old-school CPC (Car Parking Caper).

Although the hypnotism concept was very tempting, it would need to encompass the entire syndicate, making it a logistical non-starter. But it was worth noting for future reference.

In fairness, most of the ideas, apart from the dubious prayer mat, would generate funds. But overall, the majority were very risky, time-consuming, and offered small return.

So, the only two legitimate contenders were the dead donkey raffle and the old-school CPC proposals.

Dead donkey raffles are apparently age-old, simple to perform and involve little outlay.

In fact, the only four requisites to make this work were a book of raffle tickets, a non-existent prize, a spurious reason for its non-availability and refunding the winners' stake money.

The monies taken for all the other ticket sales are 'in the bank'.

The possibility of this working seemed very dependent on selling enough tickets and the winner's gullibility and disposition. Recalling to memory Humph's 'Orfapaedic' mates, Dave was sceptical about it being a contender.

The second option, the old-school CPC, required the purchase of a hi-vis jacket, a leather satchel, a sheet of card (without an old masterpiece attached to it), and a chunky marker pen. Its success was totally dependent on finding a large area of vacant land.

The ideal location was close to a railway station, an airport, or any major event.

The trick was to make a low-priced, cash-only, all-day parking sign, wear the satchel and 'official' looking hi-vis jacket and use a vehicle as 'bait'.

This would create the illusion of an official-looking car park with an attendant and one vehicle already parked.

Once the area was full, remove the sign and skedaddle with the cash.

The two real issues with this scenario were finding the land and the possible intervention of the legal landowner.

However, because of its short duration and element of surprise this may reduce or even eradicate the chances of the latter concern becoming a reality

Joe resolved the first issue when he said that he was sure that Foggy knew of a large unused piece of empty land located quite near to the mainline station.

It could be a goer!

However, things changed when George returned to the room and threw a spanner in the works by proposing that Dave should visit his bank manager, who was also his accountant. "He'll arrange a non-repayable loan to clear the entire debt."

That obviously grabbed Dave's immediate attention and he asked what the catch was.

"No catch. If you successfully undertake a task for me, it repays the loan in full."

"If it involves any criminality, then I'd be crap," said Dave quite adamantly.

"Join the club," said George, panning his arm around the room.

Looking directly at the whiteboard George continued and professed that his jobs were less effort than the CPC, "Which I'd lay odds is the one you're considering."

As he was so accurate with his supposition, maybe his offer was the best one to pursue, and whatever the degree of risk it was without doubt the most expedient solution.

"I'm interested: how do I start the ball rolling?" asked Dave hesitantly.

"Go and see Greg and he'll sort you out a WIIFU."

As Dave noted the name Greg in his phone, George continued to explain that Greg was not his real name, but his nickname acquired through his appetite for sausage rolls.

Handing over a business card, he advised Dave to meet

Greg at a club that he owned called Pluto's – "He'll sort you out!"

Dave was again slightly perturbed to be meeting with yet another villainous type who was going to be 'sorting him out' and by the fact that cosmic coincidence had re-arisen.

Ignoring both anxieties, he continued and he reiterated the name Pluto's as he typed it into his phone.

"Yeah, as in the underworld god – not the cartoon dog.

"That's Scooby's, my other club in Marbella.

"Pluto's in the town centre, near the old marketplace, and fatefully for Greg, just along from the bakers.

"Greg's there most nights, and if I were you, I'd go tomorrow. It's a safe bet that he'll be there – well, a lot safer bet than your last one!

"No offence.

"I'll get word for him to expect you."

As he stood up to leave, George revealed that there was also a secret entry code that Dave would need to get into the club.

He leaned forward and whispered that "On Tuesdays it's the rhyme, '*I'm a little teapot*'. You'll need to sing it, and perform the actions, after inhaling the contents of a helium balloon.

"No rhyme, no funny voice, no entry and no WIIFU.

"You'll be back to square one!"

He then leaned back, firmly shook Dave's hand and turned towards the exit.

Accepting that the club name was Pluto's, he braved challenging George over the entrance ritual being bogus, with an optimistic plea, "You are kidding about the rhyme!"

"Sadly, for you, I'm not," laughed George, twisting his body to undertake a comical teapot gesture, "don't forget the helium or you won't get in!"

The door then slammed, and he was gone.

In his anxiety, Dave had forgotten to ask him what a WIIFU was.

Chapter 10

It's A CONtract

ON THE RETURN journey, Dave's voice filled the car with many questions, the most important being whether anyone knew what the hell a WIIFU was?

As no one did, he abandoned that line of enquiry, and probed the vicar (now he was at it!) about the criminal activities of the inmates they'd just met.

"Well, with the exception of George, they're all petty criminals and most of them are more than a sandwich short of a picnic!"

"Well I thought that some of their ideas were quite creative," said Joe.

"Their creativeness has got nothing to do with their brains, it's because they're all scheming dodgy bastards," boomed the vicar, and his body vibrated with laughter.

After a moment he settled down and continued his appraisal of the inmates. "Ali, prior to emptying the company safe, was a senior accountant. He tried to escape justice by blaming his actions onto the controlling mystical power of his ancient prayer mat.

"Denzel, or Dense Al as he's known, is in for shoplifting. He really did fall off the turnip truck!

"He truthfully believes that the coloured sand inside of

seaside glass souvenirs are the cremated remains of clowns' ashes, and he also thinks that the House of Commons is a brown sauce factory.

"He even managed to convict himself, with overwhelming CCTV evidence.

"He was recorded stealing goods whilst looking directly into the camera to claim that the store was being robbed by the invisible man.

"It emerged that a mate had told him that using Vaseline would blur his face and make it unidentifiable on security cameras.

"Instead of smearing Vaseline onto the camera lens he rubbed it all over his face."

The cabin erupted in laughter and the vicar simply said, "What can you do?

"Even his trial judge told him that if sentencing was in line with stupidity, he'd be getting life."

Again, his large shoulders jiggled up and down in sync with his hearty laughter.

"Basically, the bloke's a moron!

"Ned scratched a living as a backyard wrestler until he decided to branch into burglary. His thieving ways were cut short when he posted an online selfie.

"He uploaded a picture that showed him posing with a 'cute' pet parrot that resided in the house he'd just burgled... and when interviewed, the parrot was able to give police his full description!"

More hearty laughter filled the car.

"He didn't really, I made that up!

"The homeowner saw it on Facebook, and Ned got nabbed.

"Tosh went off the rails at quite an early age, after his father underwent gender realignment and became his mother!

"He was very psychologically damaged, and he turned to the church for support, which the lead from the roofs, the

83

contents of community chests and valuable ecclesiastical arte-facts provided him with, until he also got caught!

"George is the only serious career-minded criminal amongst them. He's doing a ten-year stretch for his part in a safety deposit heist.

"The contents are still waiting to be found.

"He considers himself the 'guvnor', Top Cat, and a cut above all the others in there.

"He's savagely sarcastic and he can be abrasive, but really, he's more brain than brawn, unlike some of his associates!

"You know that one of his associates got banged up for feeding ducks."

"Harsh," said Joe.

"Not really – he fed them into a petrol-driven woodchip-per. Their owner owed George money!"

"REALLY?" blurted Dave.

"Yes, REALLY," said the vicar.

"So, with that in mind, give me a good reason, why I should pay his banker-accountant mate a visit?

"You know, the one who sorts people out?"

"You mean, apart from endorsing the agreement with George to do so?" said a more serious-voiced cleric.

"I don't think I did," said Dave.

"You shook hands, didn't you?"

"Yeah and…"

"Well in George's book, that's your signature, you've agreed to honour the arrangement."

As the proverbial penny tumbled, Dave grasped the fact that George wasn't a 'good' Samaritan and he said, "Well Zip-a-Dee-Bloody-Doo-Dah, thanks for that," and went into a sulk.

Attempting to lessen the impact of George's *fait accompli* and improve Dave's mood, Joe said, "Well I'm not an expert, but as Greg still seems to be a bona-fide bank manager, they tend to be more daylight than violent robbers.

"I'm sure everything will be OK!"

Dave piped up, "It sounds more like a 'contrick' than a contract. I wish I'd plumped for option two."

"Well, why not do both?" said Joe. "I'd be up for a lark, and I know that Foggy's always game! We could meet in the morning and take a drive out to sus out the suitability of Foggy's parking plot."

"Now it sounds more like an Ealing comedy," roared the vicar. "The Lady Killers, if I'm not mistaken. As much as I would love to get involved, you'll understand if I don't," he said, tugging at his dog collar.

He then issued a warning to Dave, that whichever course of action he was going to pursue, he should not miss the meeting with Greg as "it won't be the healthy eating option, if you catch my drift."

"I gathered that from the duck story," said Dave, "and I've no intention of missing the meeting."

As the words left his mouth, Dave thought to himself *that having more than one string attached to the 'Operation Make Good' bow could prove to be a wise decision.*

Arriving back at Joe's house, they thanked Reverend Black for organising their visit, and they stood and watched Moira's smoky ass disappear out of sight.

"See you at ten tomorrow?" enquired Joe.

Dave tentatively confirmed, "Yeah, I'll see you at ten."

Chapter 11

Spamdemonium

ARRIVING HOME DAVE headed into the kitchen, where he flicked the kettle switch and sparked it into life. He opened the freezer, and randomly selected a ready meal, removed it from the packaging, and bunged it into the microwave.

Ironically, it was a Chili CON Carne!

After the timer ping, he removed and scooped the cooked meal into a bowl, grabbed his mug of coffee and perched both precariously onto the desk in front of his computer.

Launching his email, he observed that the subject header on the top one read:

AN URGENT COMMUNICATION
FROM THE FEDERAL BUREAU OF INVESTIGATION.

"Yeah – of course it is," he said out loud, laughed and with two clicks of the mouse he consigned it to spam.

Moving further down the list a message from eBay also caught his eye.

On opening it he read:

Important message from eBay seller central

Reference item: 0001357328641159931 / FREE MONEY

The above item was posted with a buy it now price of 59cents.

This item has violated US federal law and the FBI have issued instruction that all such listings be removed by eBay.

We have therefore supplied The FBI's internet fraud unit with your details, and in certain circumstances they may email you.

Should they do so, we must advise of the upmost importance to fully comply with any requests for information or documentation.

Please ensure you respond within the specified timescales, as failure to do so could escalate the matter into becoming a more serious offence.

You must cease and desist from further listing this type of product on eBay otherwise your account may be suspended or permanently closed.

The eBay team – seller central

In shocked disbelief Dave stood up and, without removing his gaze from the screen, began twiddling his forelock with his fingers.

His initial concern was how the hell his item had ended up on the USA site when he felt sure that he'd only posted it as a UK listing.

As all trace had now been removed by eBay there was absolutely no way of finding the answer.

Placing the palms of both hands onto the desktop he tapped his thumbs and gently swayed back and forth, as he stared quizzically at the screen.

After a moment, he smacked his forehead with the palm of one hand, accompanied with the vocal realisation that he'd binned the poxy forms.

How the hell was he going to contact the effing FBI?

He hastily typed FBI into the search engine and the official site link appeared. Clicking on the relevant heading took him straight into the homepage of the Federal Bureau of Investigation. Dave quickly peered along the top headings and was bemused to see one called 'fun and games'!

Really, he thought.

After locating the contact button, he found that it accessed several points of contact, either to a field office, an overseas office, or the head office – bloody hell, this was getting scary.

No idea, I guess – start at the top, the head office.

He composed his email explaining the situation and asked if the forms could be resent.

Ping and it had gone. *Jesus, I hope that's not an extradition offence*, he thought.

An automated reply bounced back.

> **Thank you for contacting the Federal Bureau of Investigation, an operative will review your enquiry and respond presently.**

His nightmare had just got worse.

Chapter 12

The Falacing Act!

NEXT MORNING AFTER checking if he'd had a reply from the FBI, which he hadn't, he set off to Joe's.

He announced his arrival by once again pounding the brass knackers against Joe's door. It was Foggy who answered, and he gave Dave one of his characteristic 'Wotcher' greetings.

Before entering Dave, pointed at the **Bun Id Ye Ho** house sign, and asked what it meant.

"Behind You," chortled Foggy, and not realising that it was the answer to the anagram, Dave turned round to look behind him.

Foggy repeated the answer and this time it registered with Dave.

Mystery solved, they went inside and through into the kitchen; it was Joe who was in residence.

"Morning, Dave," he said, handing over a freshly brewed coffee.

"I've brought Foggy up to speed and he's in!

"He's going to direct us to the spot I mentioned yesterday."

"The spot is spot on," said Foggy, prior to grinning and noisily slurping a gulp of coffee.

"The plan is, coffee, visit the area and if suitable and you're up for it, we can go and buy supplies. Sound like a strategy?"

"It does to me," said Dave.

"Not only is it the ideal area," said Foggy, "I also happen to know the owner. I used to hang out with him back in our demo days. I know he won't mind us using his land for a few days – your troubles are over!"

"Brilliant!" exclaimed Dave. Things were almost legal and looking up.

After locating and inspecting the site, it proved to be the ideal spot for the CPC money-making scheme.

So, agreeing to a musketeer-type pact, they headed back into town to buy the necessary items to 'set up shop'.

They parked in one of the town's more select supermarket parking spaces and decided to 'do lunch' instore.

"It's on me," exclaimed Dave, grateful for the help with the morning's work.

"Never been in here before," said Foggy, browsing what he liked to call the 'Me and You'.

"I'm pleasantly surprised, I was expecting to see pheasant and quail egg paninis, Sultan's golden cake and carbonated Vatican spring water."

"It's not that exclusive," said Joe, "with the exception of course of the Vatican spring water."

"Really?" said Foggy, re-scrutinising the menu for the unusual mineral water

While they awaited their orders, Dave flicked a napkin open and asked Foggy how things were with him and Miss Yueh.

They all found this remark quite comical and laughed out loud.

"It went very well," said Foggy and with a twinkling eye added, "we're practically an item."

After casting a doubtful glance at Dave, Joe said he had some fond memories of an American Asian delight called Phat Phuk.

It was a Vietnamese noodle restaurant in Las Vegas.

The convivial atmosphere continued throughout lunch, after which Dave checked his phone for emails – particularly anything from the FBI.

Fortunately, there was nothing.

So, after skinny lattes and flat whites they left to find the art shop to get supplies.

Arriving at the art store there was a commotion outside the music shop next door.

It transpired that a musician had asked a female assistant if she would let him have the sex in the shop window.

Horrified at the request, she'd pressed the emergency counter alarm and summoned the community police.

The officers were attempting to calm a visibly irritated Dutch musician, who was vigorously gesturing towards a saxophone in the window display.

In the time it took to purchase the items for the 'project', the fracas outside had subsided and cleared.

They visited two more stores and purchased the remaining items they needed; now they were all set to get their CPC up and running.

On their way back to the car they crossed paths with a group of 'hensters' who were carrying a variety of saucy balloons.

This prompted Joe to recall that Dave needed to buy a helium balloon for his meeting with Greg.

"You need one of those," exclaimed Joe, pointing in the direction of the flimsily-clad women.

"You're not wrong there," said Dave.

"Not the girls – the balloon," said Joe.

"You need it for the helium to get entry into George's club, remember?"

"I'd blanked it out," said Dave. "Where do you think they got them from?"

"One way to find out," said Foggy, and he disappeared towards the giggly gaggle.

Moments later he returned with his face dappled in smudged lipstick.

"Friendly bunch!" exclaimed Foggy.

"They said they got their balloons from a shop called LOONS just up the road."

They briskly set off to find it.

After a few minutes, they discovered LOONS – a 'bijou' store selling party balloons for all occasions!

"Well I guess this must be it," said Joe, now making his way towards the glass entrance door.

As he reached for the handle, he noticed there was a hand on the other side of the door about to turn the open sign to closed.

Acting instinctively, he gave the door a forceful shove causing the shop assistant to smack her knuckles and stumble back.

Stepping inside Joe apologised, "Sorry, luv, but we urgently need to buy one of your helium-filled balloons."

The woman explained that she was closing early as she was low on balloons and gas.

"There's an extraordinary abundance of hen parties in town tonight."

Joe reiterated the importance of Dave acquiring a balloon!

"It doesn't matter what it is, anything inflated will do."

The shopkeeper said that she would see what she had left in her stockroom, and then disappeared through a tiny doorway.

Moments later, she emerged carrying a deflated sausage-shaped balloon. "I can inflate this, it's all I have left," she said.

"That's fine," said Dave stepping aside to let her get access to the gas bottle.

Attaching the balloon to the nozzle she turned the tap and it started inflating, but within moments the gas spluttered and stopped hissing.

She quickly knotted the end to stop the gas from escaping

and apologised. She then offered them what was clearly a partially inflated set of genitals.

"Is there anywhere else that we might get a balloon from?" queried Dave, embarrassed and disturbed at the sight of the deflated donger.

"I'm afraid not, the last girls who came in said that I was the only one in town who had any balloons left.

"If it helps, you can have this one for half-price."

"We'll take it," said Foggy decisively.

"Have you got a bag?" asked Dave imploringly.

"I have," and after stowing it inside a clear plastic bag, the deal was done.

Outside Dave felt even more embarrassed at the purchase so he removed his sweatshirt and placed it inside the bag to hide the offending acquisition.

He made it to the car without incident and, after ferrying Joe and Foggy back, he drove home.

Again, after an email check confirmed there was still no communication from the FBI, he grabbed a quick shower, ate a sandwich, and set off to keep his appointment with Greg.

Chapter 13

E,I,E,I,O

BACK IN TOWN Dave navigated his way through a cluck of boisterous hen parties and he eventually found George's club.

He approached the entry phone system mounted on the wall beside a foreboding large black door, and he timidly pressed the button.

A broad Scottish voice growled from within the perforated steel box.

"Friend or filth?"

"Friend," stated Dave in a nervy reply. "George sent me!"

"If that's true, then you'll know the entry routine!" declared the raspy cigar smoker's voice.

Taking a couple of steps backwards and looking all about him to check that he wasn't being observed, he untied the knotted balloon and inhaled several large gulps of lung-filling helium.

Then in THE most hysterical voice imaginable, he began the rhyme.

> "I'm a little teapot short and stout
> Here's my handle – here's my spout
> And when I get steamed up, I just shout

'Tip me over and pour me out' –"

Pausing in the desperate hope that he could stop singing the rhyme at this point, unfortunately for Dave, the voice from within had other ideas and it bellowed for him to keep going.

Dave continued:

> "I am a special pot that is true
> And here's an example of what I can do
> I can turn my handle into a spout –
> Tip me over and pour me out!"

During the routine he had remembered to enact all the actions and when finished he also added an involuntary bow, which made him feel even more stupid.

An explosion of laughter erupted through the speaker unit and the Scottish accent just audible above it invited him in.

A loud buzz and a clunk of the electronic door bolt signified that he'd passed the test.

Embarrassment made him make an exception to his littering rule and he threw the deflated balloon onto the pavement and entered the club.

On the other side of the door a large-framed individual stuck out the statutory villainous big hand to greet Dave.

"Welcome to Pluto's, I'm Greg."

"I'm Dave," exclaimed Dave in his still high-pitched cartoon voice.

As they walked across the floor Greg said, "You won't know this, but last time I visited George, he bet me that he would get a total stranger to come here, inhale helium, and perform and sing 'I'm a little teapot' to gain entry.

"I didn't for one minute expect such an individual would exist let alone cross his path – so I took the bet.

"Then what do you know – you fucking turn up!"

That's me alright, thought Dave, *I'm the gift that keeps giving!*

"By the way, wasn't that a giant cock that you were sucking the gas out of?"

Dave now felt even more uncomfortable and was way, way, out of his depth.

"No, NO way, that was a hotdog, it was all they had left in the shop!"

Greg raised his gaze towards a large screen on the wall and steered Dave through a crowd of uncouth-looking characters and into a room located behind the bar.

The large screen was obviously attached to the entry system as it was replaying his excruciating entry performance.

Thankfully, the crinkled deflated genitalia were totally indistinguishable as such.

Fixed to the door of the office was a sign that read 'EIEIO'. "What's that stand for?" asked Dave pointing at it.

"My surname's MacDonald and even though I don't own a farm it amused these buggers enough to nail that to my door."

Once inside the cat-swinging chamber that Greg called his office, he gestured for Dave to sit on one of the crushed-velvet beer-barrel seats.

Greg proceeded to wriggle himself into a leather captain's chair, located behind a chaotically-laden desk.

As he fidgeted into it, he managed to disrupt the symmetry of all the wall hangings by brushing them with his back.

One of the larger frames tilted and nearly slid off its hook and onto the floor. It contained a poster depicting the image of a pair of weather-beaten wild west saloon bar doors, with the words LAST CHANCE etched into the top of them.

Greg leaned over and straightened it, then said he understood that Dave had come to collect a WIIFU.

"Am I right?"

"Well if I knew what a WIIFU was, then you could be!"

"Before I can answer that," said Greg, clearing a space on his desk to rest his elbows, "there are a few security questions that I need to ask you."

He proceeded to source a scrap of blank paper and retrieve a pen from under the pile of documents that he'd just shoved out of his way.

"First question, are you known to, or wanted by, the police?"

Thinking that this might not be the best time to mention the FBI incident Dave looked Greg fully in the eye and confidently answered, "No."

"Would you say that you are a fast driver?"

"I'm definitely not slow," said Dave.

"Can you ride a motorcycle?"

"Haven't done for a while but yes, I can."

"Are you good at keeping secrets?"

Having still not mentioned the FBI to Greg he felt truthful in answering, "Yes."

"Have you ever fired a gun?"

"Only at the fairground."

"Can you operate any industrial equipment such as a high-powered pneumatic angle grinder, or a diamond coring drill?"

"No," said Dave in some dread of the next question.

"Lastly, are you familiar with the term Leggett?"

"If you're referring to scarpering, then the answer's yes."

Greg finished jotting down the answers and with an animated flourish stabbed a concluding full stop into the sheet.

Following a quick review, he opened his desk drawer, removed a large stapler and a blue cardboard folder, and then unsuccessfully attempted to staple the scrap of paper onto it.

After several failed attempts, and in a fit of pique, he directed another question to Dave.

"Can YOU tell me of ANY good uses for a stapler that doesn't work?"

Before Dave had time to respond Greg had launched the stapler into a metal waste bin and then responded to his own question by saying, "There aren't any."

Closing the folder containing the paper scrap, he said that he passed security and could now tell Dave about a WIIFU."

"A WIIFU's a **what's in it for us** task-related repayment loan.

"It's like a bank loan, except we're more up front with our terms and conditions.

"They're generally sought after by those who drink in there," he said, pointing up at the saloon door poster that he'd just straightened.

"Also, for health and safety reasons, *primarily yours*, I'm obliged to tell you that WIIFUs do contain some severe penalty clauses. But on the plus side, if things go to plan, they are fully non-repayable. You simply agree to undertake a task set by George and once fulfilled to his **complete satisfaction**, the loan is paid into your bank account and, it's yours to keep!

"What if I fail with the task?" croaked Dave.

"You won't," said Greg, in a light-hearted yet quite intimidating manner.

"You won't!

"No one ever has!"

"Is it OK if I get some mates to help with the task?"

"As long as they know that WE'RE NOT paying for their services, and that they're NOT PLOD, then we don't have a problem."

So thruppence being half of sixpence, task it was!

After signing the documentation, a firm handshake, and a promise from Greg that he would be in touch soon, Dave was back in the street and heading for home.

Along the way he again checked his phone for emails and as there was still nothing untoward maybe he was in the clear?

It was to be an untimely start tomorrow, so an early night was in order.

Chapter 14

They Spoked Too Soon

IT WAS JUST after dawn when Dave steered onto the dew-sodden turf of the would-be parking site; he and Foggy went about setting up while 'Jo' said she'd wait in the car.

As Dave put on the jacket and threaded his head through the satchel strap Foggy strategically positioned the large sign for maximum exposure.

It was not long before a stream of weary-looking commuters started driving onto the field, and the area began to fill quite quickly.

Foggy walked towards Dave, and after dragging on a freshly-lit spliff he raised his thumb and said, "Winner winner..."

Mirroring the thumbs-up gesture, Dave responded by saying, "Chicken dinner."

However, in time-honoured fashion, they had both spoken, or in this case, spoked too soon!

As the words left Dave's lips, the arrival of an extended chrome-spoked front wheel attached to an ear-shattering Harley Davidson, turned the lucky saying into a dog's dinner.

On entering the field, the Milwaukee marauder was deliberately driven straight at their parking sign, which it very effectively demolished and ploughed into the muddy turf.

The troublesome perp then proceeded to aim his snarling machine directly at Foggy and Dave.

They looked on in frozen disbelief as it was brought to a halt just prior to collision.

Behind the handlebars was a muscly, heavily side-burned, moustached figure, whose name, according to the legend emblazoned on the back of his jacket, was PSYCHO, and he was a member of a Hells Angel chapter called the Magpies.

After silencing the intimidating motorcycle Psycho jerked it backwards and propped it onto its stand.

He trudged over to Foggy and Dave and menacingly informed them that they were on their site. "You're trespassing on our land."

"Whose land?" asked Dave.

"The Magpies' land, you tosser!

"They ain't going to be 'appy to find you 'ere!

"So, I suggest you SOD off before they arrive!"

Emboldened by his herb, Foggy retorted by saying,

"And what if we don't sod off?"

Lifting the corner of his waistcoat, Psycho exposed a knuckleduster, a sizeable sheath knife and what looked like the twin metal nostrils of a double-barrelled shotgun.

After the reveal, he poked himself in the chest and said, "One for sorrow," clearly referring to himself as the lone magpie.

"Not if you salute it," said Foggy.

The look on Psycho's face indicated that NOW might be the optimum time to 'SOD off'.

Grabbing hold of Foggy's lapel, Dave proclaimed that they were leaving, and he frog-marched Foggy to the car and swiftly drove from the field.

As they sped away, Foggy turned and through the back window he gave Psycho the middle finger.

"What the fuck are you doing?" yelled Dave catching sight of the deed in his rear-view mirror.

"I'm saluting Mr Magpie."

By now the distinct throbbing sound of approaching motorcycles could be heard rumbling in the air.

"They don't own that land," said Foggy.

"I really don't give a fuck," squawked Dave. "If they said they owned the sun and they wanted to levy a daylight tax, I'd pay them!"

"But they don't own it," said Foggy, "it belongs to my mate Boggy.

"He's probably there now hugging a tree or tunnelling underground."

Looking anxiously into the rear-view mirror, Dave responded, "Unless Boggy wants to hug his maker, let's hope that he stays hidden until the poxy Magpies decide to sod off!"

Jo simply said, "Amen."

Chapter 15

Daily Bread And Nuts!

WITHIN A SHORT drive, Dave's pulse stopped racing, as did his car, which for some inexplicable reason had suddenly become sluggish and was beginning to slow of its own accord.

This coincided with a squeaking noise and a strong burning smell, which seemed to be coming from under the bonnet.

As puffs of smoke filtered through the air vents and into the car Dave blamed the cause on "being a bit too eager to leave the field,"

"That shouldn't have caused a problem," said Jo. "I think you'd better pull over and investigate."

As the car got slower Dave steered towards the kerb, but before he managed to park safely, both the engine and power steering stopped working.

This caused him to mount the pavement and almost collide with a mobility scooter that was being driven along it.

To add insult to injury the scooter driver aggressively bashed his heavy wooden walking cane onto the roof of Dave's car and yelled out a tirade of obscenities as he sped on by.

"That was embarrassing," chirped Foggy.

Instantly, Dave was reminded of the old woman who had kneed him at the bus stop:

What is it that makes old folk so bleeding aggressive?

After popping the bonnet catch, Dave began tentatively lifting it. Foggy and Jo stood either side of him, anxiously watching.

As Dave lifted it higher, they could all see there was a smouldering grey woollen 'thing' tangled around the fan belt and flywheel.

"What the hell is that?" enquired Jo.

"It's a blanket, a frickin' woollen blanket," said Dave, tugging out some of the shredded pieces from around the fan belt.

"It's my old man's fault, he always told me to cover the engine if the temperature dropped and I forgot to remove the bloody thing this morning."

"Where did your old man park his car – in the frozen Siberian wastelands?" said Jo sarcastically. "No one covers their engines these days."

"My old man does!" retorted Dave.

Foggy interjected to say that he'd also be a victim of some duff cold weather advice. But his was courtesy of a radio weather forecaster, who'd advised that anyone planning to travel in the icy conditions should take a shovel, blankets, extra clothing, four hours' supply of food and drink, and a reflective triangle with them.

"I don't mind telling you, I felt a complete prat on the bus that morning."

That was exactly the tonic Dave needed; the tall tale had not only improved his mood, but if true, it also lessened the embarrassment of his predicament.

The over-blanket incident had not gone unnoticed and it was not long before it attracted some passing attention.

"I've heard of cooking food on an engine, but never your bedding," said a willowy white man sporting bright ginger dreadlocks.

He was carrying a loaf of brown bread under his arm which had a dog collar and lead attached to it.

"Well obviously, you haven't lived," said Dave contemptuously.

"Especially not in the frozen wastelands of Siberia," said Jo.

Both he and Foggy high-fived and blew a spurt of laughter.

Without giving a second glance at either Foggy or Jo, the man leaned forward and stooped over the engine. As he did, he inexplicably placed the loaf of brown bread onto the top of the engine and proceeded to ask it – "What do you reckon, boy?"

After a few moments, he stood up, removed the loaf, put one end of it to his ear, then relayed the fact that the loaf had advised him to tell them that the gate spring had come unhinged!

He bent down, gently placed the loaf onto the pavement, and walked off dragging it behind him.

Dave looked at Foggy and Jo, who like him were in total bewilderment at what they had just witnessed.

Things became slightly clearer after a middle-aged woman stopped and after looking Jo up and down, exclaimed, "I see you just met The Gingerbread Man and 'Ovis'.

"He's totally bonkers, but harmless enough. Believe me, there's a lot like him round here."

Again, she scrutinised Jo in wide-eyed bemusement.

"Well, it takes all sorts," said Dave, suspecting from the clothes being worn by the woman that she might also be cast from a similar mould.

"If you're talking all sorts then that's Liquorice Lenny," said the woman.

She then unexpectedly lifted her leg, bent her knee, leaned sideways, and let out an enormous fart, "Sew a button on that," she said and walked off chuckling.

"A button – more like manhole cover," said Dave wafting the air with a chunk of the scorched blanket.

The two events had encouraged him to extract the remnants of the blanket with extra vigour, and after recovering and dropping the last of the mangled fragments onto the road, he slammed the bonnet shut and suggested they get out of there.

The other two didn't take much persuading and they quickly followed Dave back into the car.

A sharp turn of the key and the car was back to full power.

They were mobile again… "What the hell's a gate spring?" said Dave.

"Dunno," said Foggy, "but it's not the only thing that's come unhinged around here."

Chapter 16

Lenny's Extra Special

AS THEY JOURNEYED back towards 'Normalville', Dave felt a hunger pang and the need to make up for the breakfast that he'd missed having been up since silly o'clock.

"According to the sat nav there's a fast-food drive-through just along here. Fancy it?" he asked.

"I could go a Mediterranean Turkey Slider," said Foggy.

"A what?" said Dave.

"A Mediterranean Turkey Slider," repeated Foggy, "I saw it on the 'me and you' at that supermarket yesterday."

"Really! You really fancy that?"

"Not really," said Foggy.

Driving just a short distance further on, they spotted a sign not too dissimilar to their own car parking creation. It was the outline of a large arrow, inside which was written "Home-made **Bergers**'.

"Let's hope they cook better than they spell," said Jo.

However, two important factors justified Dave's decision to continue to follow it.

The first was that it was pointing in the same direction shown on his sat nav, and the second was hunger!

His desire to eat superseded any doubt in its suitability due to some minor misspelling or possible sabotage.

So, he drove on to find it.

Moments later, Jo spotted and pointed out a large sign up ahead.

It read: '**Burger Me**'.

"Bit rude," said Dave.

Driving closer revealed a partially-lit neon sign and that the full name of the diner was **Burger Meister**.

Dave considered a lengthy queue of cars a good sign, and it was moving along quite quickly.

As they neared the order point, Dave noticed a scruffy male wearing a classic Rasta-style red, gold and green hat, and he was sauntering purposefully towards the car.

The bright-eyed figure made a circular motion with his hand to indicate that he wanted Dave to open the window.

Dave pressed the window button and to appear tough, he hoarsely uttered the word, "Alright,"

The relaxed figure nonchalantly responded by saying, "Blessings, me bredda," and he continued speaking in a curious style of patois.

"The Babylons take me wheels so me can't drive-thru to get brefast and I and I is an 'ungry man.

"Will you get the 'ungry man his brefast?"

"Can't you eat in?" asked Dave suspiciously.

"I lass me job for blazin'," and he pointed to a roll up tucked behind his ear.

"T'ree years boxin food and they ban I from the building."

On seeing Jo, he gave her a broad flirtatious smile, which quickly turned into a startled, confused look.

He held out a mangled £5 note to get him a meal. Dave took the money and said that he would add his order to theirs.

"Raspect bredda, aks for the Lenny special with EXTRA cheese!

"Don't forget the extra cheese."

He said, "Kool," fist-bumped Dave and ambled off to be at the front of the queue.

Dave looked at Jo, then Foggy, whose only comment was if Dave thought he might be Liquorice Lenny.

Lifting his shoulders to express uncertainty, Dave drove forward and barked their order, along with the Lenny special into the speaker.

The voice from the unseen universe asked if there was anything else.

Dave didn't recall hearing the extra cheese addition so he repeated, "EXTRA cheese with the Lenny special."

He drove forward to occupy the space beside the service window.

After a few moments, another voice relayed back the order including the Lenny special with extra cheese.

After confirming it was correct, a hand attached to a tattooed hairy arm stretched through the open window and presented a collection of brown paper bags.

Dave promptly pulled them into the car, passed them over to Jo and hastily drove forwards.

However, in his eagerness to move the car, the orders all became jumbled and no one had a clue as to what was in each bag, or which one contained the Lenny special.

Before they could decide, the "ungry man' had appeared at the side of the car to collect his order.

Quickly scanning the bags, Dave noticed that one had a totally different colour scheme to the others, so he presumed that it had to be the Lenny special.

He slowed to hand over the food and as he did, he was unceremoniously and aggressively hooted from behind.

After grabbing the brown bag, the now not-so-relaxed "ungry man' made towards the offending car behind yelling, "Why are you vexing me man?" He then got embroiled in an argument with the driver.

This altercation proved timely and fortuitous, and it provided Dave with the ideal opportunity to jog on without having to get further involved with either Lenny or his special.

Chapter 17

Things Are Getting Fishy!

DAVE'S STOMACH BEGAN frantically signalling his brain that there was food waiting to be eaten, so he was relieved when he spotted a brown sign pointing towards a picnic area.

After seesawing the obligatory speed humps, he parked close to an unoccupied wooden picnic table, which they commandeered and dropped their collection of brown paper bags onto.

"Let's see what we've got in here," said Foggy, using both hands to pull open the top of a randomly chosen bag of food.

As the sides of the bag unfolded, he tilted his head to peer inside, and somewhat startled by what he saw he handed it to Jo and he made a facial gesture to look inside. After Jo looked inside, she held the open packet in front of Dave's face.

"You're joking," said Dave, gazing into a bag full of money!

He promptly grasped hold of it and closed the top of the bag.

"It must be the Lenny friggin' special," said Foggy.

"Well if it is," said Dave, "I've now got a rude boy AND a murder of magpies on my case."

"Don't forget Humph," chortled Foggy.

Jo said that she thought it was odd that Lenny was so insistent about adding the extra cheese, but after having seen the contents of the bag it prompted a recollection that 'cheese' was the urban word for cash.

"It just gets better and better," said Dave, burying his face into his hand.

"Let's not worry unduly," said Jo. "IF the contents of that bag are the ill-gotten gains of a burger heist, in the unlikelihood that we should ever come across the 'ungry man again we simply act dumb.

"We can deflect suspicion by insinuating that his accomplice must have double-crossed him as our bags only contained the food that we ordered.

"As for the Magpies, they're not after US!"

She specified the word 'us' with a hand gesture indicating she was referring to herself and Dave.

"If I recall, I believe that it was Foggy who saluted Psycho."

Jo laughed then put a reassuring regular-sized hand onto Foggy's shoulder and said, "Only joking. They're not interested in any of us."

That pep-talk did help ease Dave's mind and the situation didn't appear quite as bleak as it first seemed.

Perhaps if push did ever come to shove then maybe some of George's 'wildlife' associates could take care of the "ungry man', the Magpies, and, if all else failed, maybe Humph as well!

Feeling less anxious, Dave sat back down at the table and drew the bag containing the 'fillet of funds' back towards him.

Foggy and Jo both started to consume the food, which prompted Dave to hold aloft the bag of money and say, "I'll eat this, then."

Without reply, Foggy ripped open his brown bag, tore his burger in half and placed it along with a clutch of fries onto the torn packaging. He then slid it in front of Dave.

Declining the mullered offering, Dave unfurled the top of the tightly closed bag and carefully inserted his hand inside to remove its contents.

He withdrew a substantial clasp of notes and both Foggy and Jo repositioned themselves to provide cover, whilst he counted it.

Dave said that it added up to £500.00, and right on cue the voice of Fred Flintstone yelling 'Yabba dabba doo' sounded from Dave's phone.

He picked it from the table and answered it, and after a pause said, "Hi, Greg."

After attentively listening, Dave asked if a text could be sent, the reply was obviously no, so he said he needed to get a pen and paper.

Foggy hurriedly emptied bits of lettuce and cold fries from a burger box and tore the sides open to make it into a writing surface, and Jo searched out a pen.

Dave cradled the phone between his shoulder and his ear and began to jot down instructions, pausing only to enquire as to the spelling of certain words.

After filling most of the packaging with details, he concluded by saying, "That's fine... I'll collect it this afternoon... yes, I'll go this evening." He then ended the call.

Both Jo and Foggy looked eagerly at Dave in anticipation of hearing his news.

Dave asked if they fancied a trip to the seaside. "It's the job for George."

"Depends on the job," said Jo warily.

"Well, I've got to go to a specialist garage called Camel Towing, find 'the mechanic' and collect a van.

"I've then got to drive it to a place near Skegness and collect some exotic fish that George has bought from a bloke called Andy *Aquatillian.*"

Dave checked his notes and corrected his statement, "Collect from Andy at Aquatillian.

"I've then got to deliver the fish to a 'Zookeeper's' house in Thetford."

"And is that it?" asked Foggy.

"Apart from not feeding the fish, as the Zookeeper's taking care of that, that's it!"

"What about the name of the garage?" queried Foggy. "It sounds like a wind-up to me!"

Dave rechecked his jottings and replied, "That's what he said."

"Did he specify what kind of fish they are?" asked Jo.

Again, referring to his telephone minutes he said, "Pygo Natty something or other, they sounded rare."

Jo asked Dave if he thought the name might be *"Pygocentrus nattereri."*

"Could be," said Dave.

"Well if they are, and memory serves me correctly, that's the Latin name for Piranha."

In the short time of knowing Jo and her alter ego, one of their common traits was the ability to recall an encyclopaedic amount of incongruous facts and trivia, so, there was every likelihood that she was right.

Apart from the fish and the outrageously-named garage, Jo said the errand sounded quite harmless, and she'd love a trip to the seaside, so count her in.

"Me too," said Foggy.

After the burger bonanza and George's activation of the WIIFU, at last, things seemed to be genuinely on the up!

Whilst Foggy and Jo cleared the table and ripped the packaging into untraceable shreds, Dave stuffed the money into his trouser pocket and went back to the car to tap 'the mechanic's' address into his sat nav.

After getting rid of the 'evidence' into several different bins, Foggy and Jo joined Dave in the car.

While they waited for the talking roadmap to find its voice, Jo confessed that apart from Butlin's, which became HMS Royal Arthur during the war, Donkey rides and a John Hassall railway travel poster, she knew very little about Skegness!

Sounds like a very lot to me, thought Dave.

Suddenly a sound resembling a surprised elephant trumpeting through the jungle came from the back seat.

It was Foggy blowing his nose on an enormous tissue.

Looking on in astonishment, Jo asked Foggy if he hadn't bought a box of paper tablecloths instead of tissues.

"Manly," said Foggy, holding the large box aloft so Dave could see it in the rear-view mirror. Foggy then went on to convey his Skegness trivia, which revolved around the type of rides that his mates operated at Butlin's and along the sea front.

"That's not the job it used to be," said Jo. "I believe you need five O-levels to become a *Fairground operative* these days."

Once again, she had ably demonstrated her retentive capacity to recall odd information.

Foggy decided to put Jo's knowledge to the test by asking her if she knew what a 'purple nasty' was? "It was a question in our pub quiz last week."

Jo responded and told him that it was "Half of lager, half of cider and blackcurrant cordial mixed in a pint glass. It's more commonly known as a snakebite."

"You're good," said Foggy in genuine admiration. "And to answer part two of that question, is it illegal to sell a 'purple nasty' in a UK bar?"

"I think that's an urban myth, started after President Clinton tried to order one in a Harrogate pub. The landlord told him it was illegal to serve!

"So, my hundred per cent answer would be it's not illegal!"

"You should go on a telly quiz programme," said Foggy, even more awestruck by Jo's knowledge.

As they continued to discuss whether Jo should, or would, join Foggy's quiz team, the sat nav came to life and it issued the command to **turn left and continue straight for 4 miles.**

After voicing his opinion that snakebite might make a great limited-edition sales promotion for Cobra beer, Dave jabbed

at one of the radio's pre-set buttons, and the sound of Bobby
Darin singing 'Mack the Knife' began reverberating inside the
car.

When that shark bites, with his teeth babe, scarlet
billows start to spread…,

Jo remarked about the coincidence, and Foggy said it was
either that, or another bleedin' omen.

"**Don't start all that**," said Dave, cricking his neck round
to give Foggy a furrowed brow and faux-menacing glance.

Foggy responded by clicking his fingers and joining in the
chorus.

The spontaneity of the action was infectious, and both
Dave and Jo were compelled to follow suit and they all
growled out the words in unison adding in a few YEAHs for
good measure.

With the car bouncing in song and good humour, they
journeyed on towards another 'Operation Make Good'
exploit, and as the route took them near to Jo's home, Dave
made a detour in order that she could change her outfit.

Chapter 18

How Not To... Cross A River

ONCE 'CHANGED', JOE was back on board, and the sat nav led them through a mystical warren of side streets and eventually navigated them to some Godforsaken backstreet where Del Boy again proclaimed that they had reached their *destinashun.*

The road contained a long row of railway arches that were now housing a diversity of businesses.

The place was as muddled in sight as it was in sounds, and after parking, Dave hoped that this really wasn't going to be as scary as it appeared!

He informed Joe and Foggy that Greg had said that they were looking for a blue building and as they were outside a blue building – so far, so good.

Opening the car door, he suggested that Foggy and Joe wait while he went and checked things out. "No point in us all getting mugged."

He removed the ignition key and handed it to Joe.

Joe and Foggy watched on as Dave weaved his way through a multitude of cars and vans and over to a side door in the blue building. He opened it and disappeared inside.

After what seemed an eternity the door of the building reopened and a forebodingly large, shaven-headed man was leading Dave back outside, and he pointed towards a building further down the road.

Dave nodded, and shook his hand then started back towards the car.

He was carrying a large carrier bag in his hand.

Dave got back into the car and explained that it was the wrong building – "That's a printing works" – and, raising the bag, said that he'd got some samples of their work.

"What were they printing?" asked Joe.

"Money," said Foggy, only half-joking.

"You're right," said Dave, dipping into the bag to retrieve a bundle of imitation ten- and twenty-pound notes printed as novelty serviettes.

"There's your Humph solution," said Joe.

"Yes, and if he wouldn't accept the notes in a bundle, I could always supply them on a roll," said Dave, fishing out some novelty printed toilet rolls containing the same ten- and twenty-pound note designs.

He passed the bag to Joe and said, "It's that darker blue building over there, the one with the 'Scammell Towing' sign."

"Not Camel, then," said Joe, jocularly slapping his thigh. "That's pure Panto gold!"

"You literally made a twat of yourself there," said Foggy in unanimous merriment.

After a few moments' drive they were pulling up beside a large wall-mounted 'Scammell Breakdown Recovery' sign and, confident that this was the right place, all three of them left the car.

As they walked towards a narrow inset shuttered doorway, Foggy told Dave that he'd phoned his cousin in Skegness and she was going to organise free digs for their overnight stay.

"Top woman," replied Dave exuberantly.

They entered through the doorway and found themselves

inside an oily, petrol-smelling abyss, and the whole place was a hotchpotch of vehicles, all in varying stages of repair.

Foggy tugged the door shut and it made an ear-clattering sound.

A grubby set of pink dungarees emerged from beneath a hydraulic ramp supporting a precariously perched car.

It was a robust blue-haired woman who was filling them.

Wiping her greasy hands on a rag that she was carrying, she sauntered towards them.

By the look on their faces she felt compelled to say: "Yes, I am a woman.

"Yes, my hair is blue, yes, I am a qualified mechanic and for your information, yes, I own this garage.

"Anything else you'd like to know?"

"Got a name?" asked Foggy.

"It's River, but everyone calls me…" and before she could finish the sentence, for some bizarre reason Foggy said, "DYKE!"

Although Foggy had said it in an under-his-breath whisper, the capacious shape of the brick building amplified his comment and the accompanying sniggers and River received it loud and clear.

Standing immediately in front of them, she looked extremely displeased; she was also a lot bigger and more intimidating than she had appeared from a distance.

Prior to responding to the glib remark, she grabbed a large chrome spanner from the floor, looked them up and down and began forcibly smacking it into the palm of her hand.

After several taps, she suddenly hurled the spanner against the wall, and it rebounded into a large battered toolbox.

She then targeted a piercing gaze directly at Foggy and said "They call me White Water.

"Not because I'm a native American, but because I'm turbulent, unpredictable and extremely dangerous to cross, so if I wanted shit from you, I would have squeezed your head."

She then forcefully prodded Fogy's chest, causing him to step back, and said: "WANKER!"

"This is my workplace," she said, pointing around the building. "I don't come to yours and spit on the burgers. TWAT!"

"I'm sorry, luv," said Foggy, "I think you might have misheard and have got hold of the wrong end of the stick!" but before he could introduce the fictitious misheard word *pike* into the equation, River dealt him another cynical blow.

"What stick would that be then, that twiglet in your pants you call a penis?" she scowled at him and said, "and don't call me love!"

She was clearly, and most definitely, not amused!

To try and placate the situation and move on, Dave said that Greg had sent them, to collect a van.

"Greg says a lot of things."

River strode over to a small table that was strewn with greasy motor parts, she picked up her mobile phone, scrolled the screen then tapped it.

When it connected, she informed the contact that when they'd said crew, she wasn't expecting Captain Pugwash and his seamen! Having reiterated the word 'seamen', she cast another disdainful glance in Foggy's direction.

After a pause, whatever the reply it genuinely made her laugh out loud and she blew a raspberry through her lips.

She continued the conversation by confirming that the van wouldn't be ready in time.

Listening to the response she answered, "OK, I'll give them that," and she ended the call.

After a final penetrating stare at Foggy, she held out her hand and said, "River, AKA White Water, AKA the Mechanic."

In turn they shook her hand and, like scolded infants, each sheepishly announced their name.

"Follow me, there's been a change of wheels!"

She turned and guided them through a small brick archway and into an even more cavernous area.

Like the first workshop this one was also strewn with a jumble of vehicles and spare parts.

In one corner there was a noticeable large blue tarpaulin and River made a beeline towards it.

Once they were all assembled beside it, she vigorously tugged back the tarpaulin to reveal a Wallace & Gromit-style motorbike and sidecar. The sidecar had a Perspex hood and a spare wheel attached onto a small chrome luggage rack that was fixed to the back of it.

On seeing it Dave felt that he should be commenting, "Cracking good job, Gromit!"

But after River's earlier reaction, he thought it wiser to leave it as just a thought.

Although it looked as if the combo had seen better days, River assured them that it was more than capable of undertaking their task and said that in line with George's requirements she'd also introduced a few modifications.

"You'll notice that the interior of the sidecar doesn't have a seat and is sealed with a watertight lining. The front nose cone is also detachable.

"That knob at the back," she said, pointing to what looked like an oversized blue gobstopper on a chrome stick, "pulls back to open the cone and pushes forward to close it.

"We've found it the easiest and safest method of transporting some of George's more unique cargo."

That sounds ominous, thought Dave.

"We once transported a Komodo dragon in this baby and believe me, you don't want to be trying to lift that mother out.

"The registration number's printed onto a magnetic panel," and to demonstrate this fact she peeled it off and then reapplied it.

"You'll need to remove it before you gas the swan. George wants it brought back here."

Before they could ask, River continued, "I've made several carburettor adjustments, so you need to treat the throttle with respect and whatever you do, don't touch this red button, unless of course you have the need for speed. REAL SPEED!

"The guys who used to do George's banking – found it very beneficial, till they got nabbed."

Unscrewing the petrol cap, she indicated that the tank was filled to the brim. "You'll have enough here for the journey and gassing the swan!"

As she screwed the cap back on, Dave took the opportunity to pose his earlier unasked question: "What exactly is 'gassing a swan', and why do we have to do it?

"I'm not comfortable about killing anything, and particularly anything that belongs to the Queen."

Clearly not surprised at their lack of unlawful knowledge, River enlightened them as to the meaning and method of 'gassing the swan'.

"After delivering the merch, you'll need to find a discreet spot to permanently dispose of the wheels by torching them.

"George wants them untraceable and permanently gone.

"You do know what torching is?"

They all replied with nods and grunts.

"WELL in the trade, we call that 'gassing the swan'!"

Fully aware that she was dealing with an inept bunch of criminal virgins, she began playing them like a yo-yo.

"It's not a 'Bloody Tower offence' – Strangeways, maybe!"

Although the prison was no longer called Strangeways, she knew that they wouldn't know that, and would be intimidated by the notorious name.

After digesting the name and the potential consequences of getting caught, the job now seemed incredibly real and worryingly daunting.

River continued by pointing at the petrol tank and suggested that a lighted rag stuffed in there always does the trick.

Thank goodness she's explained that, thought Dave, gratefully accepting the crumbs of knowledge casually brushed from the criminal top table.

"I'd also advise that you light the rag AFTER you've put it into the tank."

"Should you get stopped at any time, which I feel sure you will, the bike's registered to a company called GVH London, it stands for Getaway Vehicle Hire, which like the names of his clubs, is George's idea of humour.

"If asked, you simply say that you hired the bike from GVH and nothing else; I'll give you all the relevant paperwork which you'll need to return along with the number plate.

"Whatever happens, if you get any problems, under no circumstances contact Greg direct.

"You contact me, I'll give you the number.

"Should you need to call, you refer to the garage as the Bakery, to me as the Pastry Chef, Greg as the Pie Man and George as the Master Baker; clear?"

They all nodded and answered, "Clear."

She then removed and handed over a roll of banknotes from her dungaree pocket.

"Here's a ton. It will cover ONE trip back after gassing the swan, so don't go doing it miles away, or on our doorstep, I'm sure you'll find somewhere suitable between the two!

"It's also to cover any **unforeseen circumstances or emergencies**, and I will be expecting change."

That was spooky, thought Dave, *these were exactly the same two factors that had got him into this mess in the first place!*

"It's not a meal allowance, then?" he said, attempting to lessen the fear of being involved in the hazardous deed.

"That depends on whether you consider 'eating' an emergency," said River.

"You wouldn't know what type of fish we're collecting?" asked Dave.

"Knowing George, they're probably Piranhas, and by

the way, you're collecting them for 'Diamond Geezer', not George; it's his eBay tag."

Joe conveyed a 'bleeding would be' expression.

"Did Greg mention the Zookeeper?" asked River.

"Yeah, he said he'll be feeding the fish," replied Dave, totally innocent of any villainous implication.

"Well, unless one of you wants to sleep with the fishes, there'll only be room for two of you on the return journey."

A dealing-with-idiots smirk crept across her face.

"The wheels will be ready for seven; I won't be here, so follow me and I'll show you where they'll be parked."

She turned and led them back through the arches and into the main workshop.

After pausing at a large set of metal filing drawers she withdrew, handed over the paperwork and tapped her contact number into Dave's phone.

They left the building and walked across the yard.

As River passed Dave's car, she spotted the banknote toilet rolls laying on the back seat.

Knowing that the items had come from the 'wrong' building, she couldn't resist crafting another Pugwash jibe by saying, "Shiver me timbers, lads, looks like you've got a faulty sextant and a messy poop deck."

Without riposte, Dave continued to follow her to the designated parking spot, and Foggy and Joe got back into the car.

As he clicked his seat belt into position, Joe commented, "You touched a wasp's arse there, she really doesn't like you!"

"Touched a raw nerve, more like," said Foggy.

"Methinks that lady doth protest too much!

"She's a bushwhacker!

"One hundred per cent!"

The driver's door opened, and as Dave slid into the driver's seat, he just caught the last few words.

"Well, speaking of wacky bushes," he said, "from the

fragrance wafting around the back, I'd say that someone's got quite a few of them maturing close by."

"She's a charmer and competitor," said Foggy.

Chapter 19

Incy, Wincy...

IT WAS 7PM sharp when they returned and parked their car in the allotted spot.

Finding the combo parked in the specified location, they noticed there was a selection of weatherproof clothing and helmets inside the sidecar.

Closer inspection revealed it to be a diverse collection.

There was denim, leather, and suede garments, and the crash helmets looked like they belonged in a museum.

They were a cross between a helmet worn by a First World War German infantry soldier and an early American baseball player.

"It's the latest in retro biker gear," said Dave.

They began changing into the weatherproof gear.

Flexing his shoulders and moving his elbows in circular motions, he turned to Foggy and asked his thoughts on them passing as members of a chapter.

"Well, I feel like a member alright," said Foggy, trying to squeeze into some tight-fitting clobber.

Feeling that Foggy wasn't up for the venture, Dave responded by declaring, "You don't have to come with us, it's not compulsory!"

"It is," said Foggy. "If I don't go, then my cousin won't let you stay at her friend's place.

"My mates are also expecting me to be spending a few days working with them."

"How are you getting back?"

"With this," said Foggy, raising his thumb.

"So why are we staying at a friend's place and not your cousin's?" asked Joe.

"Cos she lives in a tiny caravan."

Joe said that for him space was never a problem.

And having seen the pictures of Joe performing the P&J show on Brighton beach, Dave could believe that.

Whether it was a swanky hotel that served *Kopi Luwak* or a cramped caravan that served black pudding, so long as there was clean bedding, a working toilet and hot water, then he'd be happy.

"What the hell's *Kopi Luwak*?" asked Dave, trying to force his legs into some tight-fitting leather trousers.

"It's one of the world's most expensive coffees," said Foggy.

Joe obviously knew the answer, but he was intrigued as to how come Foggy knew it.

Fascinated to find out, Joe pressed him for the answer, to which Foggy replied, "Backpacking in Indonesia.

"After a day's work collecting Civet poo, to make the *Kopi Luwak*, you could swap the 'fruits' of your labour for a night's lodgings and a hot meal."

"I'm impressed," said Dave, now adjusting the crotch of his trousers.

"Thanks," replied both Joe and Foggy in unison.

Apart from learning a lesson in coffee, Dave was also about to be taught another in character assessment.

An event was about to unfurl that would cause Joe's refined persona to slip faster than a penguin off an ice shelf.

Being the self-designated rider, Joe had begun squeezing himself into a heavy-duty one-piece leather suit, which, unbeknown to him, was already partially occupied by a large, furry, toy spider, presumably placed there as a joke.

As his shin touched it, his body reacted as if he'd touched a high voltage cable with his tongue.

His fear was so physical that in panic and eagerness to remove the garment, Joe, literally, shat himself.

Although not funny, it was hilarious...

"For fuck's sake, that's not funny," said Joe as he watched the artificial arachnid tumble out of the leg of the leather suit.

"It's not bloody funny, not funny at all, I could have had a bloody heart attack."

"Well, judging by the state of your pants I'd say more like fart attack," said Foggy, now creased double with laughter.

Dave was trying to hold it together, but he couldn't and clutching onto Foggy's shoulder they both guffawed like a couple of 'laughing sailors' in an amusement arcade.

"I'm glad that you both find it so amusing," said Joe, ripping off his boxer shorts and flinging them straight towards Foggy and Dave.

The soiled underwear sailed through the air and above their heads, and just like a hoopla, span around and partially covered an object protruding from the top of the container behind them.

Moving closer to the mystery item Foggy could see that it was a "bleeding camera" and no sooner had the words left his mouth than it suddenly and silently moved and the pants unattached themselves and slipped onto the ground.

"Yeah, and I bet some bastard is having a right laugh on the other end," said Joe, attempting to clean himself up with a couple of white silk scarves that he'd removed from the sidecar.

"I reckon it's the bushwhacker," said Foggy, now resting his hands on his knees to support his laughter-aching body.

"Well, she can whack – er – bush with this," said Joe, and he proceeded to gyrate his pelvis and thrust his genitals directly at the camera.

"Have a basin-full of this as well…" he said, turning around to complete the display with a moony.

He then resumed cleaning himself up.

After more throaty laughter-coughs and cuffing-of-laughter tears, Dave and Foggy simmered down and regained their composure.

Joe finished cleaning himself up and blaming the incident on the bike, he furiously threw the scarves at it.

Moving over towards the spider, he aggressively stamped on it and booted it across the yard, then he bent down to retrieve the leather suit.

"You're not going to wear that?" asked Dave sceptically.

"Why not?"

"Well, if the fact that you've crapped in it is not a good enough, reason then… why not?" said Dave.

"Good," said Joe, forcefully sliding up the front zipper of the hastily reapplied suit.

At this point they were all fully attired and ready to roll.

Putting their civvies in the sidecar, Foggy squeezed inside and Joe straddled the bike.

Dave asked Joe to wait for a moment and he nipped back to his car.

Retrieving his key that he'd tucked beneath the wheel instructed by River, he unlocked the car and removed the three-dimensional and hanging air fresheners.

After attaching the hanging air fresheners onto his scarf so they dangled just a few centimetres away from his nostrils, he returned to the bike.

As he mounted the pillion seat, he deliberately slipped sideways, so as he could grab Joe's shoulder and adhere the wobbly headed air freshener to his back.

Once on-board Joe pushed the start button.

The engine roared into life.

With a tap on the gear pedal and a twist of the wrist, their next adventure had begun.

Chapter 20

The Open Road...

AS THEY HEADED toward the A1, Foggy pulled himself upright using the handle behind the sidecar wind deflector. Due to this action Dave suddenly realised that they'd left the Perspex canopy behind, and, concerned about possible repercussions, he hollered out the fact.

"Too late for that now!" shouted Foggy, sitting upright and he theatrically raising his arm to recite a quote from *The Wind in the Willows*:

"The whole world is before us – we're on the open road."

"Let's just hope we don't end up crashing out as spectacularly as Toad did," said Joe, giving the throttle a small twist and causing Foggy to slide back down into the compartment.

"That was and still is one of my favourite books," said Foggy.

"And I'd say quite appropriate," said Joe.

As the bike purred along, Dave was thankful that whether it was due to the wind direction or the air fresheners, so far, there had been no untoward odours radiating from Joe's direction

Even the warm oily petrol vapour drifting from the hot carburettor was not unpleasant.

Give it a few miles and perhaps he could dispose of the pine-smelling baggage hanging around his neck.

"I bet you can't guess what my favourite book is," said Dave, inviting responses.

"Linda Goodman's *Sun Signs*," said Joe, quick as a flash.

To which Dave retorted, "Ha bleedin' ha!"

"*Fever Pitch*, Nick Hornby?" answered Foggy, equally swiftly.

"How would you know that?" said Dave, genuinely flabbergasted.

"A bit of a giveaway," said Foggy, pointing to the bobble-headed Arsenal footballer stuck onto Joe's back.

Still unaware of its existence, Joe piped up, "And I think I'm right in saying, 'For alarmingly large chunks of an average day, you are a moron'.

"Am I not?" said Joe, quoting a line from the book.

"Not quite," said Dave. "It's 'I am a moron'."

"That's what I said, didn't I?"

Shaking his head at Joe's attempt at humour, Dave asked him what his favourite book was.

"*Drags to Riches* by Danny La Rue."

"Really?"

"No, not really!"

"It's *Alice in Wonderland*."

On hearing this, both Foggy and Dave exchanged 'we're not surprised' looks.

The journey continued, and Dave contemplated the fact that both his travelling companions' favourite books were children's ones – which was eccentrically understandable.

It was not long before they entered the motorway darkness and had left behind them the urban landscape, (the sidecar top), and the streetlights, which twinkled and faded like distant fireflies.

The motorway was curiously bereft of any other traffic,

making it eerily quiet, and even the sound of their engine seemed muffled by the cloak of darkness.

After several miles, the calm night air was suddenly disturbed by a ferocious noise that was fast approaching them from behind.

The volume increased, which was in some part due to the darkness, but primarily because it was closing in on them.

Dave and Foggy both twisted their heads rearwards and Joe checked in the mirrors to try and determine the origin of the sound.

What they witnessed moving ever closer was not a sight for sore eyes.

What looked like a column of soldier ants was teeming up the road behind them and the closer the procession came, the more obvious it was that they were not cretaceous insects, but hirsute, bearded bikers – or Hells Angels, to be precise.

The reason for the lack of traffic also became apparent as they had spread themselves across the entire width of the road, stopping other road users from passing.

Crap, THEY were about to become an indent in the following chapter.

Chapter 21

The Manifestation
Of The Indentation

JOE, DAVE AND FOGGY suddenly became surrounded by glistening chrome and muscular tattooed forearms. The scowling machines pulling alongside them were transporting some very menacing-looking individuals.

The front riders began weaving their bikes so that they came within very intimidating proximity of the combo.

The lead biker leaned over and yelled, "What's your chapter?"

In swift response and an enhanced macho voice Joe shouted back, "We're not affiliated."

As more of the pack caught up with the lead members they too embarked on undertaking and overtaking manoeuvres which eventually forced Joe to move into the middle lane. The result of this was that they were now trapped inside a mechanical spider's web.

To make things worse, as the bikes haphazardly passed by, Dave spotted another major concern. The backs of several jackets were emblazoned with the Magpie logo.

On seeing this, he used a series of jerky sideways head and eye movements to draw Foggy's attention to the logo.

He followed this by briskly pointing into the sidecar and making a two-handed gesture towards his face, indicating that they should goggle up!

Foggy rifled about inside the footwell, attempting to locate the goggles, but the first thing he managed to retrieve was one of the scarves that had tumbled into the sidecar after Joe's spider outburst.

Vividly recalling its use, Foggy quickly threw it over his shoulder. It snared itself onto the luggage rack and unfurled and flapped like a revolutionary battle flag.

Eventually, Foggy located the goggles and handed them out.

In the relatively short time it had taken to find the additional headgear, they had been surrounded by even more bikers.

It became obvious that wherever the pulsating mass was destined to go, so too were they.

After an uncomfortable period that seemed like forever, but realistically was probably only fifteen minutes, the front of the convoy veered left. The rest of the motorcade, including them, then flowed like molten mercury into the same direction.

As they drove along the slip road Dave's mind recollected the petrifying memory of Foggy's salute to Psycho, and he prayed upon everything sacred that their paths weren't about to cross again.

Joe brought the combo to a halt in the car park and they soon found themselves surrounded by the curious and the cantankerous.

The first to pull up and goad them was a bearded beefcake who asked, "What do you three jokers call yourselves – 'The Aardmen'?" obviously referencing Nick Park and pointing at their combo.

Then, drawing attention to the bobble-headed air freshener still attached to Joe's back, his ample female passenger joined the ribaldry by asking if it was their tag.

"Looks like one to me," said another biker, who had coasted over to join the harassment.

"I think these must be the infamous Bobble Heads," he enthusiastically proclaimed.

Bringing his bike to a stop, he tilted it sideways and supported it on the rest.

Casually dismounting, he strolled over to inspect the attachment and after flicking it to make it wobble, he professed that he thought that the "Bobblehead tag" was "exclusive to us Asians."

He lowered his head to scrutinise the object closer then tilted his face sideways and commented, "Shit team, nice smell."

Raising himself back upright, he snatched hold of the bobbler and wrenched it from Joe's back!

Then, with a peck-like motion of his hand, he plucked hold of Dave's goggles and pulled them as far forward as the elastic would allow. He let them go and with an almighty thwack they snapped straight back into Dave's face.

The force made Dave reel backwards and tumble off the bike; this, along with his expression, greatly amused the gathering and it lessened the hostile atmosphere.

The goggle-snapper then turned his attention towards the back of the sidecar, and he clocked the vintage silk scarf hanging from the luggage rack.

Grabbing hold of it, he twirled and wrapped it around one hand and forcefully tugged and jerked it free and then held it aloft in a triumphant salute of his belligerent prowess.

The lack of protest or resistance from the 'intimidated' three suggested to the leather-clad audience that the show was over and there was little else to see here, so they began to disperse and re-join the main nucleus of the gang.

The chief protagonist also decided to leave and as he ambled back to his bike, he held aloft his contraband and wobbled his head from side to side.

On reaching his wheels, with a forceful smack he attached the plastic bobbler onto his front mudguard.

He then swung the silk scarf around his neck, nonchalantly straddled the seat and repositioned his sunglasses (who knows?) over his eyes.

Forcefully lugging the bike off its stand, he pressed the ignition, turned, and left.

After the scary incident, and in an insinuating tone, Foggy was the first to speak and he directed the blame at Dave.

"Thank fuck he didn't also notice the pine woodland you've got hanging around your neck."

In an annoyed retort, Dave said, "And you should thank fuck it wasn't Psycho."

Joe joined in by saying, "I think we all should thank fuck that we're still in one piece. I suggest we get the hell out of here before he gets a whiff of what's on the scarf hanging around his neck."

Using the throttle sparingly, he gently guided the combo away and, to avoid running the gauntlet again, he took a short cut through the petrol station.

Although the number of vehicles refuelling did provide cover, they also provided obstacles that he had to zig-zag through to reach the exit.

Chapter 22

The Sandman

HAVING MANOEUVRED BETWEEN several vehicles, they made it out of the sight and hopefully out of the minds of the troublesome congregation gathered in the car park.

Joe stopped the bike and leaned back to speak to Dave.

"Get on your phone and find us another route, we don't need those idiots catching up with us again."

Without comment, Dave searched, scrolled, and studied the results on his phone.

While he did this, Foggy volunteered to go and get some drinks from the garage.

After a few sharp thumb flicks on his screen, Dave suggested that they could exit the motorway at the next junction.

"We turn left at a roundabout called the Bucket and Spade and follow the B road for about 20 miles. We can then spin back onto the A16, which'll take us all the way to Skeggy."

"Unusual name for a roundabout," said Joe, scrutinising the map on the screen. He handed it back to Dave saying that it looked like "an escape plan".

Foggy came back to the combo carrying a card cup holder containing three hot drinks and a bag of food.

"We'll have the refreshments after we're out of harm's way," said Joe.

Foggy stuffed the bag into the sidecar and, holding onto the cup holder, he corkscrewed himself back into a comfortable position.

Under the garage lighting, Joe noticed just how jammed into the sidecar Foggy was, and he could not help but comment, "You look like a bleeding mollusc."

On re-entering the motorway, they raced along towards the next junction. After a significant spurt, and in the absence of any would-be pursuers, Joe eased back on the throttle.

A steep slip road off the motorway loomed ahead of them, and as they drove towards it, all three of them took an instinctive glance behind to see if they were being followed.

Apart from a shiny flame-red truck, the road behind them was clear and thankfully bereft of any motorcycles. As the lorry passed, the driver blasted a foghorn sound through a set of chrome air horns mounted on top of his cab.

Both the sound and the juggernaut punched a hole into the night air, and the oooom, oooooom, oooooooooooooooooooooom sound, elongated and distorted as the juggernaut whooshed passed them.

Once it had disappeared, they took another quick glance back: all was still well, and they were rid of any potential trouble.

The slowdown, after the tyre-blistering dash, made the approach up to the roundabout seem pedestrian, but that all changed when Joe inadvertently pressed the red booster button and the combo shot into the curve of the central island.

In an equally sharp and excitable manoeuvre, Joe wrestled with the handlebars which resulted in the combo twitching and shuddering from side to side, causing the sidecar to buck up and almost tumble over.

The drinks and several sandwiches flipped out and splattered onto the road surface.

But Foggy, thanks to the snug fit and reactive use of his elbows, managed to stay encapsulated inside the sidecar.

After another brief but frantic struggle with the handle-bars, Joe managed to regain control of the bike.

Seeing that Foggy was still in situ, Joe commented, "You really are a bleeding limpet!"

In a shaken but hardly stirred manner Foggy replied, "Easy, Tiger." He then asked, "WHERE'S DAVE?"

The pillion seat was empty.

Within seconds and before Joe could reply, a distant shadowy figure could be seen staggering along the road behind them.

There was the answer.

Joe steered the bike to the side of the road and up onto the grass verge. He disembarked and rushed towards the approaching silhouette.

As Joe got closer, he noticed that Dave's dishevelled frame was covered in yellow powder.

After placing his hand on Dave's shoulder Joe commented, "I don't know what happened there!"

"I do," said Dave. "You tossed me off."

Childish innuendo, maybe, but Dave's statement made Joe profess that although not a laughing matter, that was "a showstopper".

Employing an airport security-type frisk-down, Joe checked for signs of damage and asked Dave if he was injured.

"I don't think so," said Dave, looking totally dishevelled and startled, "but only thanks to that weird-sounding roundabout.

"There's a giant sandcastle in the middle of it. Correction, there WAS a giant sandcastle in the middle. It's now a stretch of beach.

"Thank God for eccentric planning departments!"

After a few sideways body dips and some circular gyrations of his hips and upper torso, Dave's real concern shifted to the condition of the bike.

"Are the wheels OK?"

"She's fine," said Joe, checking the front wheel, "she's perfectly fine!"

"That," exclaimed Foggy, "is more than can be said for the tea and toasties."

Chapter 23

Driveaway!

THEIR JOURNEY GOT back underway and so did the discussion regarding the food and drink.

"Let's just say this," said Foggy, snappily addressing Joe, "up to the point that you decided to turn into bleeding Evel Knievel, we were well sorted for provisions!"

Sensing that the temperature of the debate was sliding up the scale, Dave said that there was bound to be a garage along the way, to stop for refreshment.

After a few miles and as predicted by Dave, the inviting illumination of a petrol station glowed into sight.

As the entrance become visible, Joe swung the combo into it, drove across the forecourt and parked in a bay directly in front of the sales kiosk.

All three disembarked and after making use of the facilities, they bought hot food and drinks and found a small seated area in which to sit.

Dave looked much improved as he'd brushed himself down, straightened his hair and washed his face, to which a healthy flow of blood had now returned.

Turning his head sideways, he jiggled a finger inside his ear and flicked out some sand lodged inside.

"I think I could have built a small sandcastle with the contents of this ear," he professed.

"At least you've perked up," said Joe.

"Yeah, he really is the happy sandboy," said Foggy, chomping on a hot pasty.

"Not only is that funny, but it's also quite interesting," said Joe. "And I bet you don't know who or what a sandboy was."

After giving each other 'do we care?' looks, Dave shrugged his shoulders upwards and Foggy, licking brown sauce from his fingers, asked to be enlightened.

From his trivia-laden brain Joe divulged that sand boys were itinerant Victorian labourers who dug for sand on Hampstead Heath.

They sold it for cleaning pots, pans, and tools, but mainly as a covering for pubs and butchers' shop floors, which, unfortunately for them, was superseded by sawdust, abruptly ending their digging days.

The only signs of their existence are the ponds they dug out on the heath and their reference in that old saying.

"Interesting, huh?"

"Very," said a disinterested Foggy as he made his way back to the counter to re-stock on food.

"The only two things that I know about Hampstead Heath are that it rhymes with teeth and that you don't hang about there after dark," said Dave.

Just as he finished making the comment Foggy returned to his seat with a giant hot dog protruding from the ends of a bun and Dave said, "I rest my case!"

The sight of the bun along with Dave's comments tickled Joe's funny bone, making him belly laugh which left Foggy somewhat confused, but without enquiring further, he just sat back down and continued eating.

As customers for fuel and refreshment were thin on the ground, the sight of a policewoman entering the shop was very conspicuous.

Stopping just inside the doorway, she authoritatively enquired as to the ownership of the motorcycle combo parked outside.

As Joe, Dave and Foggy were dressed in leathers, and the only ones inside the store, it seemed that the answer to that question might have been obvious.

However, Joe responded by stating, "That would be us."

With his use of the word 'us' he had wilfully involved Dave and Foggy in whatever was about to follow.

Moving closer to the trio, the policewoman used her intimidating and ample presence to physically box them in, and at this proximity she looked like she'd only left school that morning.

"Who's the driver?" the policewoman asked.

"Me," said Joe, rooting in his pocket for his licence in anticipation of the next question.

After scrutinising it in a short-sighted manner, the WPC, without comment, handed the licence back to Joe.

"There's a bunch of Hells Angels congregating in the services a few miles back and there's been a spate of drive off fuel thefts reported.

"We've run the plate on your vehicle outside and although you're shown to have been at the garage, you're not on the list of suspects.

"Coincidence, is it?"

There was a silent pause from all.

"What do you mean by coincidence?" asked Foggy.

"Coincidence that your bikers and you just happened to be in the area at the exact time of the gathering. Is that coincidence, or are you part of a chapter, deliberately coming here to cause us problems?"

"Do we look like any part of a chapter?" asked Foggy.

"You do, your bike doesn't," replied the superior but now slightly less intense scrutineer.

"But you never know, we've had people in mobility vehicles cause us mountains of grief."

Tell me about it, thought Dave, recollecting the blanket incident and the stick-wielding roof-banger.

Withdrawing her notepad and pen from her top pocket, she continued.

"We did notice, after running the plate, there seemed to be a distinct lack of information about the vehicle ownership, just that it is registered to GVH London. What's GVH?"

To avoid 'further enquiries', Joe was not about to reveal the acronym, so, he simply replied by saying, "It's a specialist vehicle hire company."

"And THAT," she said, pointing out of the window at their bike, "really is 'special'." Her assessment of threat made her comfortable in taking a couple of steps backwards. This reduced tension and returned everyone's personal space.

"So why are you here?"

Foggy stepped forward, "We're visiting my cousin for the weekend."

"Where does your cousin live?"

"She lives in Skeg…" Before he could complete the sentence, the automatic sliding door zipped open revealing yet another pimply blue-clad 'youth' who proclaimed excitedly they had to go – NOW!

The policewoman stowed her notebook and pen back into her breast pocket, pointed two fingers at her eyes, reversed the action and in the manner of a priest performing a blessing, sprayed the trio with the silent watchful eye warning.

The duo then jogged off in Batman and Robin fashion towards their vehicle, and prior to the electronic doors shutting, the words… "All hell's broken out… LITERALLY," filtered back into the store.

"Thank you, Psycho," said Joe, raising his cup of tea.

Chapter 24

Ding, Dong!

AFTER A MONOTONOUS, but thankfully uneventful, couple of hours, the black tarmac of the Skegness seafront road began to rumble beneath their wheels.

Ahead was the famous Diamond Jubilee Tower, opposite which was the Jolly Fisherman statue, the rendezvous point arranged with Foggy's cousin.

As Foggy concluded a text telling her they'd arrived, Joe brought the bike to a halt.

The three dismounted and embarked on some more vigorous arm-and-leg blood recirculation movements.

It was relatively quiet and the haunting sound of whooshing waves enticed Dave to stroll towards the beach to take a closer look.

As he peered into the bracing darkness, the soothing sound was dramatically interrupted by yet another pulsating din.

Whether due to the surroundings, the quietness of the hour, or some fancy engine tuning, the high-octane decibels were loud, and the sound continued until it grumbled to a stop.

Dave turned and made towards the source of the commotion and as he drew nearer, he saw the figure of a leather-clad, raven-haired, ruby-lipped beauty, glamorously alighting from the irritable machine.

She made towards Foggy and gave him a huge bear hug.

Even though she was lithe and petite, the forceful nature of the embrace made Foggy puff out his breath, and he inadvertently spat a freshly-lit reefer onto the ground.

Without hesitation, the energetic female stooped down, swiped up the misshapen cigarette, swiftly placed it between her lips and took an immense drag.

In doing so she created a sizeable haze of fragrant-smelling smoke and shortened the tab by at least a third.

After letting the vapour drift back into her mouth and out through her nose, she handed the roll-up back to Foggy.

Not to be outdone he too produced a cloud of billowing smoke and whilst savouring the moment, he put his arm across the shoulders of the woman and introduced her as his cousin, Liberty.

Joe, being Jo, stepped forward and greeted her with the double cheek kiss, but Dave, who was embarrassingly smitten by the woman's beguiling appearance, could only muster the courage to hold out a hand and offer her a pathetic formal handshake.

Liberty ignored Dave's outstretched hand and gave him a hug.

"It's nice to meet some of Lionel's friends!"

Three things struck Dave after the greeting.

The first was the heady smell of cannabis and exotic perfume.

Secondly, was the tattoo of a bell on Liberty's neck... and thirdly and possibly most importantly, was the disclosure that Foggy's real name was Lionel.

Before Dave could pursue the revelation, Joe beat him to it.

He parodied the opening words of the Lionel Ritchie classic song *Hello*, and mockingly asked Foggy if was it him that he was looking for?

"Hysterical," said Foggy.

Dave joined in with another famous refrain and said, "I guess that's why he's easy like Sunday morning!"

Foggy was clearly not impressed by either their humour or singing ability, and he took hold of Liberty's arm and asked her to explain why she'd called him Lionel.

"Because when we played charades at Christmas, he always insisted on being team captain.

"So, we nicknamed him Lionel after Lionel Blair, captain of an old TV mime show, and it stuck."

"Mystery solved?" asked Foggy, taking another lug of smoke.

"Well if it's not Foggy, or Lionel, then what is your first name?" asked Joe.

"You'll need to get his birth certificate to find that one out," said Liberty.

From the tone of the declaration Dave suspected that it was a touchy subject, so he changed it, and asked Liberty about her bike.

"It's a single-cylinder, 4-stroke, twin spark, air-cooled 499cc 1969 Royal Enfield Bullet 500.

"It produces 28.1 bhp at 3800 rpm, has a transistorised coil multi-curve ignition system and holds the record for the longest production run of any motorcycle – ever."

"As well as for being the loudest," interjected Dave.

He was now completely in awe of Liberty; she was beauty and brains.

"It's loud because the guys I work with have supercharged it for the show."

"What show?" asked Dave.

"The 'Wall of Death'. We do a seasonal gig in Dreamland."

He then asked if she was one of the riders.

"Of course. On the circuit I'm known as Liberty Belle."

She lowered the zip on her leather jacket to reveal that the tattoo that Dave had glimpsed on her neck included the Statue of Liberty intertwining with the bell.

Ding bloody dong, thought Dave.

Chapter 25

In 'N' Outa Love!

GETTING BACK ONTO the saddle of her bike Liberty said they should follow her to the 'Che La Casa' where she'd got them beds for the night.

"From its name, I'm guessing there's a Spanish vibe going on there?" said Joe.

"More 'revolutionary'," replied Liberty as she proceeded to awaken the growler with a forceful stomp from her black leather boot.

The reply didn't make much sense to Joe, but without any further clarification forthcoming he did as instructed and followed Liberty through a labyrinth of meandering back streets.

Eventually, they arrived outside a sizeable double-fronted, three-storey property that had obviously been a hotel in more prosperous times.

Sprayed onto the wall was a selection of slogans, a 'Ban the Bomb' logo and a large silhouetted image of 'Che' Guevara which had the name 'Che La Casa' sprayed beneath it.

On seeing it, Dave suggested to Joe that it looked like his 'Am Dram' artist had stayed there at some time!

Parking their bikes next to a huge pile of wood, they ascended a steep climb of steps up to a shabby front door.

Attached to it was an equally shabby sign which read 'Come Back with a Warrant'.

Joe whispered, "I guess the odds on clean bedding, a working toilet or hot water, are looking slim."

"…and I'm not banking on breakfast either," said Dave in a hushed reply.

Liberty used her knuckles to tap out a mysterious knock on the woodwork, and after a small delay, the sound of drawing bolts heralded a response.

The door was cautiously opened and from behind a heavy-duty security chain the face of a young woman peered through the gap.

On seeing it was Liberty, she closed the door, removed the security chain, then fully reopened it to reveal her full elfin figure.

She was wearing a red beret and an array of brightly coloured clothing, which was clearly an accumulation of differing styles and eras.

The beret was fashionably tilted to one side of her head, and with little or no makeup, she looked every inch an understudy for Pygmalion's Elisa Doolittle.

Liberty was the first to speak.

"I've brought my cousin and his two friends to stay the night.

"I spoke to Zeb about it, is he here?"

The girl turned and, using an ear-rasping screech that would have made Professor Higgins succumb to a wince, she yelled out: "ZEBBBBBBBB!"

A few moments later, the stairs juddered, and the exuberant figure of a dude dressed like Jimi Hendrix joined them in the porchway.

He greeted Liberty with a hug and invited them all in.

As they were crossing the threshold, Zeb gazed back outside and noticed the combo.

"If they're your wheels," he said, "I'd advise you to park

them elsewhere. They might not be there in the morning. There's a lot of undesirables moving into the area."

The thought 'pot and black' flashed through Dave's mind.

"You can park at mine," Liberty suggested to Joe, "and I'll run you back."

Immediately, Dave realised that Liberty's offer of a return journey would give the pillion the chance of getting up close and personal, and as she was so far out of his league, the opportunity to do that really wouldn't come again.

A bit 'pervy', maybe, but hey, he was in love!

So he boldly staked his claim to move the combo.

"I'll park the bike Joe, you've done enough for today, you and Foggy rest up, while I sort it!"

Whether due to astuteness or Dave's imploring expression, for whichever reason, Joe, without comment or hesitation, held out the key.

As he grasped it, Dave's mind spun with anticipation, and as nonsensical as it seemed, he became concerned that his euphoric thoughts were seeping through his face.

He was also fretful that in his excitement, he might have inadvertently punched the air.

However, from the unperturbed expressions on the faces of the others his fears seemed groundless, so he inhaled, calmed his mind, and redirected his attention back into the room.

By now, Zeb and the others were halfway up the first flight of stairs, and Dave had to scramble briskly to catch up with them.

On reaching the first-floor landing Zeb halted to relay some important information.

Firstly, he advised that even though the lodgings were basic and contained a diverse mix of 'guests', there were house rules.

"You'll find them written on posters pinned above all the beds," he said and pointed towards one visible through the open doorway of a scruffy room.

"These rules must be noted and adhered to, and should you

decide not to do so, then even Liberty's guests will be asked to leave.

"Secondly, the only stars now associated with this old building are the ones you can see through the roof, so it's very much a hands-on, DIY, self-catering stay.

"As for remuneration, this is usually by means of agreed barter, coins of the realm or PayPal.

"But, in your case," he said, with a knowing glance towards Liberty, "your tariff has been settled."

The bitch, thought Dave, suspecting that some form of sexual barter had occurred.

Having elevated her to the status of divine goddess, the thought of her being free and easy with her feminine wiles greatly upset him.

In fact, she now disgusted him, and he hated her.

She was no longer his sweetheart and as for the return pillion journey, he didn't want to hang on to a trollop.

However, as Zeb expanded upon how Liberty had settled their tariff, Dave's unaffectionate sulk transpired to be ill-judged, childish, and unfounded.

It emerged that she'd acquired some 'fairground spoils' that had greatly benefited the commune.

These included the huge pile of firewood that was stacked outside and a couple of vintage swing boats, which they'd restored and sold for 'good money'.

In consequence, her barter account was now in credit for a significant number of guest stays.

OMG – Dave loved her again!

Yet again, Dave's erratic thoughts had ambushed his attention, and he'd arrived in a room that he had no chance of finding again!

"Did any of you bring a sack with you?" asked Zeb, with the emphasis on him already knowing the answer to the question.

As none of them wished to hazard a foolish

misinterpretation of what he meant by 'sack', it needed Liberty to clarify that he was referring to sleeping bags.

Now they were clear, Zeb received the answer he'd been expecting.

"I'm afraid we hadn't realised it was going to be quite so self-catering," said Joe, looking critically at Foggy.

"No worries," said Liberty, "I have spares in the 'eyes cream van'. Dave can bring them back with him."

Whoooohooo, thought Dave, re-enthused that not only was his trip still on, but the words spoken from Liberty's own lips had seemingly bestowed a celestial sanction on the escapade.

This prompted Dave to recall the last time that he had felt so nervously smitten by a beautiful woman.

It was way back in the days when his face had been covered in spots, and his voice had the vocal range of a chorister.

The person in question was a girl called Theresa Bill; she preferred to be known as Terri Bill, and up until now she was the most beautiful female he'd ever seen.

She was a year above him at school but left school before he ever managed to summon the courage to ever speak to her.

This was partly due to shyness and fear of rejection, partly because she was wild and free-spirited, but mainly because she had a nutty older brother who would beat up any boy who went anywhere near her.

In truth, it seemed that 'Barnacle', as he was known, just liked beating people up, and his sister was the unwitting catalyst for his favourite pastime.

'Barnacle' had earned his nickname primarily because of his surname, but it was also because of his thug-like similarities to Bluto (Barnacle Bill) from the Popeye cartoon.

His actual name was Hilary, which did shed some light on his anger issues.

Chapter 26

Liberty's Eyes Cream 'Van'

AS HE FOLLOWED Liberty's mesmerising, shapely, leather-clad figure back down the stairs, his spatial awareness was inexplicably restricted, and, on arriving outside, he still had little or no idea as to the location of his room.

Fortunately, an obliging clue surfaced as Joe and Foggy removed their civvies and overnight belongings from the nose cone of the combo, and Foggy bemoaned his ill-fortune in having to carry his gear all the way back up to the top of the gaff.

"Thought they might have repaired the lift with some of Lib's windfall!" he grumbled.

In preparation for the big climb, he declared that he needed a stogie first, which, to Dave's surprise, referred to a thin tin of small cigars that were concealed in his jacket pocket.

Joe joined him and they both drew on their burning leaves and blew spirals of smoke into the night air.

Foggy paused for a moment and suggested that Dave bring them all back some fish and chips.

"Good thinking, skunk man," said Joe in jovial agreement.

Considering Joe's happiness, perhaps the stogie's weren't just ordinary cigars?

After a couple of tries Dave started the bike, engaged first gear, released the clutch and was on his way.

At first, he tentatively followed Liberty but as he grew in confidence, he began riding a wheel's gap behind her.

They headed back along the esplanade and past the clock tower.

Passing the amusement arcades and the bingo halls, Liberty swung a left and entered the theme park.

They rode past a variety of booths and silhouetted metal frameworks, then made towards a cordoned off area constructed from upright metal corrugated sheeting.

The word 'PRIVET' had been daubed in red paint onto one of the panels beside the entrance, so he deduced that this must be the showman's private parking area.

From the spelling of the word he also presumed that the inhabitants would be some of life's less academic characters, whose alternative talents lay in the ability to spin and increase the speed of any thrill ride up to, and beyond, warp-factor puke.

There was a maze of vans, trucks, motorhomes, and caravans, all neatly parked to form an 'auto' village.

Liberty travelled past these and carried on through the main thoroughfare of vehicles and towards a medium-sized caravan parked not far from a tall cylindrical structure in the far corner.

As they drew nearer Dave noticed that this small cluster of caravans and vehicles had all been parked to form a cul-de-sac.

The caravan that they were headed towards was parked next to a shipping container. Liberty's headlight illuminated the caravan and she turned sharply and parked in front of it.

Dave pulled alongside her and could now clearly see that the cream-coloured caravan had been decorated in an array of astrological-themed icons, the prominent one being a large pair of spellbinding eyes.

Both switched off their engines, dismounted, removed their helmets and stood looking at the vintage caravan.

"Here she is!" exclaimed Liberty.

"Here's my 'eyes cream van'."

The name required no further explanation.

As he glanced at the mystical graphics, Dave was once again confused and puzzled by the relentless cosmic intrusion into his life.

They walked towards her caravan and used the upturned milk crates to step up to the doorway of her caravan.

As she put her key in the lock Liberty expanded upon its history.

"This was once the home and business of Princess Romannia, a travelling Gypsy fortune-teller, hence the splendid imagery.

"Even without her association, being an original 1964 Sprite Musketeer makes the 'van' a collectable.

"My boss Clint owns it, and as I'm the only female on his team I get sole use of it while we're on tour."

Sounds like a decent bloke, thought Dave.

As he crossed the threshold and stepped inside, the smell of history and exotic fragrant oils combined to produce an ethereal sensory experience.

Hanging between original laced curtained windows of the dimly battery-lit compartment were some framed vintage pictures and publicity advertisements relating to a Princess Romannia.

As he studied the photographs, he noted one that depicted a large wooden sign propped against the actual caravan that he now was standing in.

It read:

Princess Romannia
Descendant of Royalty
Guardian of Dynastic Secrets

Mystical Visionary
Cross my palm with GOLD
To unveil
your Past, Present and Future!
Seek advice
on matters concerning
Business, Health, Wealth and Happiness
Palmist Clairvoyant Crystal Ball Tarot Cards

Kushti Bok!

With payment in GOLD – Dave could see why you might seek her business advice.

Having exhausted his study of the wall dressings within his proximity, Dave was reluctant to venture further into Liberty's home or personal space to look at some others that he had spotted.

So, he engaged her in small talk.

Intrigued by the words 'Kushti Bok' he pointed at them in the old photograph and asked Liberty what the phrase meant.

"It's Romany for 'good fortune'," she replied.

I could use some of that, thought Dave.

"And what do you do when the season finishes?"

"Normally I would get a job as a waitress, but there's a lot more competition from students and out-of-work actors.

"I don't have to worry about that this year, because Clint has paid for us all to go with him to Africa and help recover Yvonne Stagg's buried treasure.

"He's spent half his life trying to pinpoint the location and now he's convinced he's found it."

"Who's Yvonne Stagg and what's her treasure?" queried Dave.

"Yvonne was a female pioneer in the 'Wall of Death' business.

"She was one of the first women riders and the **very first** to own her own 'Wall of Death' in Dreamland at Margate.

"In 1961 she took a 'Wall' to Sierra Leone but things went horribly wrong and she ended up burying one of her friends and her original 'Wall of Death' somewhere in the desert.

"No one knows where, and for a showman to find it would be the same as a Christian discovering the Holy Grail.

"Clint's convinced that he knows where it's buried and if he's right, we could be unearthing more than history."

"Won't it have rotted?" asked Dave.

"Well, if archaeologists can excavate intact things buried for centuries in sand, then I don't see why we shouldn't."

On that note, she lifted the cushioned top from a bench situated along one side of the laminated food table, plunged her arm into the cubby hole, pulled out three different-coloured sleeping bags and placed them onto the table.

After reinstating the seating, she pushed the thermal bedding over to Dave, declaring that they should do the trick.

Dave backed out of the doorway and waited whilst Liberty flicked off the lights and locked the door.

"I'll stow my bike and run you back on yours, you can secure the sacks in the sidecar."

Dave did exactly as he was told, ensuring that the bags ate up most of the sidecar space and left him with the pillion seat.

Liberty strolled over to a neighbouring caravan and spidered her fingernails against the door.

As she stepped back, the top half of the door swung open to reveal a rugged sun-tanned head nestling beneath a cowboy's black hat: her boss, Clint.

There was a small cigar in the corner of the mouth and the guy had all the appearance of a wild west gunslinger.

Unfortunately, his extremely broad West Country accent instantly shattered the illusion.

"Hiya, Lib, yer be putting 'er back yonder, then?"

"Yeah," said Liberty and she turned to point her slender finger in Dave's direction.

157

"This is my cousin's mate, Dave; I'm going to park his combo here tonight after I've run him back to Zeb's place."

Clint and Dave both raised acknowledging looks at each other.

The bottom half of the door then squeaked open and clutching a large bunch of keys the full figure emerged, and until he spoke again, he was Clint Eastwood!

"Alright, me luvver," he said and proceeded to walk over to the container.

"That dawcock ner showed up to paint that privet hedge on the fencing."

"I think he's still working on the ghost train sign," said Liberty.

As they moved out of earshot Dave asked Liberty what a 'dawcock' was.

"The same thing as twat. Clint often uses it, but usually with a mixture of more colourful language.

"He thinks the painter's too talented to be decorating metal sheets to look like hedges.

"The site owner wants 'to beautify the utilitarian spaces' and make them less conspicuous."

In the light of the entrance sign having been correctly spelt, Dave's conjecture regarding the literacy of its creator almost certainly made him a 'showmanist'.

It was fortuitous that he hadn't shared his thoughts or passed them onto others!

As Clint wheeled Liberty's bike into the container, Liberty retrieved her helmet from the back of it and strapped it securely on to her head. Before they rode off, Clint handed Dave a voucher for a discounted breakfast at Butlin's.

"More than you'll be getting at Zeb's Place," he said wryly.

While thanking Clint, Liberty had started the combo and she indicated her intention to test its performance by revving it off the counter.

Dave boarded and gently clasped his hands either side of Liberty's slender waist.

He should have gripped a bit less timidly, because as she released the clutch the acceleration caused him to release his grip and slip backwards. Had it not been for grabbing hold of the luggage rack on the sidecar, he would have shot off the end.

He hauled himself back into place and this time clasped his knees extra tightly into the bike's framework and planted a firmer pair of hands around Liberty's waist.

He had a feeling that, with the exception of the roundabout incident, this journey was going to be a lot more exhilarating than Joe's.

He wasn't wrong.

As they sped up the promenade, Liberty, like Joe, accidentally discovered the red booster button, but unlike Joe, after pressing it, she managed to keep control of the combo.

As it shot forward, Dave's hands and knees automatically gripped securely onto anything that might avoid him being dislodged for a second time.

Within a short distance, Liberty disengaged the boost button and the combo slowed to a lively but more acceptable speed.

Liberty tilted her head backwards and yelled, "That's impressive!"

Within no time, Dave was back at the accommodation and after his great anticipation of the journey, the swiftness of their return had made it too quick to savour.

After a hug, the diminishing sound of the combo faded into the distance, signalling that Liberty was gone.

It was all over before it had even begun!

He consoled himself in the fact that he had at least managed to get further with Liberty than he had with Terri, and that there was always tomorrow.

He wearily trudged up the entrance stairway clutching hold

of the three sleeping bags, and as he stood at the front door, it dawned on him that he'd forgotten the fish and chips and forgotten to memorise the secret knock.

He removed his mobile phone from his pocket and was about to ring Joe when he noticed that he had a missed call from the Pie Man, AKA Greg.

It had been eight minutes ago, which coincided with the timing of Liberty's inadvertent deployment of the red retro booster button, so it was little wonder he'd not heard the ringtone.

He pondered a moment and recalled River clearly telling him that under no circumstances should they ever contact Greg direct.

Perhaps it might be wiser to go inside and seek counsel with the others, before responding to Greg's missed call.

He phoned Joe's number and waited for a reply.

Chapter 27

Wannabes, Drunks And 'Ackers'

A VOICE SOUNDING like a pantomime dame responded. "Joe," said Dave, apprehensively, and following a throat-clearing cough, Joe sounded like Joe again.

Dave told him that he was on the front porch, and that he'd also missed a call from Greg.

"Well, I'd call the Cupcake, or whatever it is she calls herself. I'll come down to let you in." Dave hung up and called River.

"Hi, you've reached the Bakery, leave a message."

"Hi, it's Dave, I've a missed a call from the Pie Man, you said not to contact him. So, I'm calling you… It's Dave."

A few seconds after ending the call his phone rang, it was River.

The voice on the other end said, "Is that Dave Dave, so good they named you twice?"

Dave tilted his head and phone skywards, succumbing to yet another cynical broadside, and then replied "Yeah, this is Dave, I just missed a call from the Pie Man."

"It wasn't Pie Man, it was me that was calling you," said River.

"I must have picked the wrong phone off the bedside table,

tell that to your mate Soggy, he can put it in his bong and do whatever he likes with it.

"I'm ringing to tell you the Master Baker's bought a van and as you've got your 'shipmates' with you, he wants you to collect and bring it back to the Bakery.

"Fortunately, it's not far from the zookeeper's place, so that's a bonus!

"He's also agreed that you'll deliver a package for the seller.

"I'll send you a pic and all the details. It's paid for and you can use some of your pocket money to tank it up.

"Only contact me again if the wheels come off the van – literally – and speaking of things coming off, I found the sidecar cockpit!"

"Oh yeah, I was going to tell you…" Before he could finish, River rudely ended the call.

Dave tucked his phone back into his pocket just as the front door opened.

Joe opened the door and his first comment was to ask Dave why he was bereft of their fish and chips.

Fortunately, the ding of the incoming text diverted the necessity for an immediate reply.

As they walked into the hallway Dave took out his phone and opened the message. It contained the image of a three-wheeled, tiny spearmint green truck, a contact name, and a collection address.

"It's from River?

"You called her, then?"

"Yeah, she was phoning to tell us we've got an extra job to do for George, and she wasn't best pleased that we left the sidecar top in the car park."

Turning his phone screen to show Joe the image, he said, "We've got to collect this and drive it back to the garage – sorry, Bakery!"

"He's really got some chutzpah," said Joe, taking hold of the phone.

"And, whatever chutzpah is, which one of us do you propose tells George that?" asked Dave.

Ignoring the retort, Joe expanded the image, and declared, "Nice, that's a classic, it's a Piaggio scooter truck."

Handing back the phone, they started up the stairs, and Joe again asked, about the lack of food.

Dave stated that the journey back had been quicker than candy floss being blown along in a hurricane, so requesting a food stop wasn't an option.

"I also had an overwhelming desire to hang on – Once bitten!"

"Oi – that was an accident," said Joe

"I did spot a burger van parked down the road that was open, we could all go there to get some grub."

As they walked along the first floor landing an open doorway revealed a flickering, aromatic-smelling room in which Zeb was sitting cross-legged beneath a large poster of Buddha.

The wording on the poster read '**Keep Karma and Karry on**!'

Zeb had his eyes closed and was gently humming while holding his finger and thumbs together, in what they were to learn was a meditative hand position called a *Gyan Mudra*.

They tried to discreetly pass the open door, but Zeb had sensed their presence, and he opened his eyes and curtailed his mantra.

After inviting them in, he proceeded to unfurl himself and get to his feet. He inhaled and exhaled a large gulp of air, and then extolled the virtues of OM and Mudra Meditation.

Having been invited into Zeb's inner sanctum, Dave was more interested in the room than the ruminations and he couldn't resist the urge to log its contents.

There was an interesting array of paraphernalia scattered about, but a shabby wooden frame propped up against the wall drew his interest.

It contained a yellowing front page of The Norfolk Times displaying a bold headline that read: '**E.T. SEEN IN SKEG- E!**'

Obtaining Zeb's permission, he moved to take a closer look, and after lifting it from the floor he saw that it was dated 5 October 1996.

The article reported sightings of strange red and green rotating lights seen floating in the sky over Skegness.

Having been witnessed by residents, police officers and the Great Yarmouth coastguard, reporters decided to contact scientists at Jodrell Bank Observatory for an opinion.

They verified that it was the planet Venus causing all the extra-terrestrial excitement and confirmed that the planet was also the number-one culprit for most UFO sightings.

Interesting – and yet again, another astrological event was crossing his path!

As he propped it back against the wall, he noticed a flowery sign with the words 'Kushti Bok' hand painted on it.

"I saw that earlier today," Dave said, pointing at it.

Echoing the interpretation that Liberty gave, Zeb also said it meant 'good fortune'.

"Well, it will be Kushti Bok if that burger bar is still open at this time of night," said Joe.

Zeb responded by telling Joe that Al's Cowboy and Indian was open all night.

They were about to leave the room when Foggy's shabby figure appeared in the doorway.

"Thought our food might be getting cold by now," he said.

"It's not even got hot yet," said Joe, "Dave forgot it, so we're going out to eat."

The debate as to whether Dave had forgotten food or not continued right up to the approach the fast food wagon.

Above the counter a colourfully lit neon sign read '**AL's Cowboy and Indian**', and like moths to a flame it had attracted all the usual suspects: the boozed, the boisterous and the barmy.

The Anglo-Asian owner introduced himself as Al and asked what he could do them for.

"If you're hungry I can recommend 'The High-Falutin' Cowboy and Indian'."

They accepted his recommendation and seated themselves at one of the sets of white plastic garden furniture reserved for customers.

While they waited, a highly polished limousine displaying a 'Jolly Fisherman's Cab Co' logo turned in and parked.

The driver got out and made his way towards the counter.

As he passed Dave he paused and discreetly asked all of them who they thought he'd got in the back of the cab.

As inconspicuously as possible they tried to catch a glimpse of the obviously famous occupant, but it was impossible to see, and they had to confess that they didn't know.

Eagerly awaiting the driver's big reveal, they were amazed to hear him say that "It was a question, not a statement," and that he didn't know either!

"I know the voice but can't place the face, I think she might be an actress."

"What makes you think that?" asked Joe, a little more interested.

"Cos I drive her from the theatre to her hotel every night.

"Whoever she is, she's got good taste in late-night food. It's the third time we've stopped here this week.

"Who doesn't love a cowboy 'all on'? And I've got to tell you guys, Al makes the best 'all on' this side of Dalston."

After placing his order, he sauntered back to the Limo, opened his door and spoke with his passenger.

Returning to the van he grabbed an empty seat and drew it near to their table. He sat down and introduced himself as Frank and said rhetorically, "I wish I could think who she is."

"There's a simple way to find out," said Foggy.

"And that is?" enquired Frank.

"Ask her!" said Foggy.

"Can't do that," said Frank, handing Foggy a business card. It read: 'our driver's integrity guarantees your anonymity'.

"We're under strict instructions never to ask questions!

"Mind you, even if I knew who she was I wouldn't remember. I have a problem recollecting names and faces."

"That's called prosopagnosia," said Joe.

"What is?" said Foggy.

"The inability to recognise faces, it's a syndrome."

"He's under starter's orders and... he's off... AGAIN," said Foggy, cynically referencing another factual gem spouting out from Joe's lips.

Picking up on the racing analogy, Frank exclaimed that 'starter's orders' reminded him of an embarrassing and valuable lesson he'd learned in people misjudgement when he first started cabbing.

"I picked up a bunch of school kids from the station and refused to drive them anywhere until their parents joined us.

"Turned out, they were all jockeys attending a two-day seminar.

"Who'd have known?"

"Joe!" said Foggy.

Dave joined the conversation by asking Frank if he was from Dalston.

"Yeah, I was a black cabby."

There was a witty reply to the grammatically incorrect statement, but Dave decided to ignore it, and ask if he'd picked up many 'slebs' when he worked in London.

"I'm not much of a stargazer, and with my syndrome I wouldn't know, would I?" He nudged Joe and laughed.

"However, if it's true, my most famous fare was probably the bloke who claimed to be the voice of the Daleks in Doctor Who.

"I have to admit, his impression didn't sound very convincing, but I got his autograph, just in case.

"Mind you, I lost it when I moved up here.

"So, whoever he was will remain an eternal mystery."

"Why'd you leave London?" asked Joe.

Frank answered by saying, "Wannabes, drunks and 'ackers'."

"'Ackers'?" queried Joe.

"Yeah, Acker Bilks – runaways, nonpayers."

"Sounds like a nightmare," said Joe. "I couldn't think of any better reasons to leave."

"How about throwing a tourist and their luggage into the Thames?" said Frank ominously.

Before they could ask him to elaborate, Al called Frank's order and he sprang to his feet to collect it.

Returning from the counter, he shook Foggy, Joe and Dave's hands and told them to be lucky.

He returned to the limo, handed the container over to his backseat passenger, whoever she was, started the car and glided off.

Within minutes of the limo's backlights majestically fading into the night, Al hollered out to say the three 'High-Falutin' Cowboy and Indians' were ready.

These consisted of steak, egg, bacon, mushrooms, peppers, and cheese, each served in a bun with a side portion of Bombay potatoes.

While they ate, they told Foggy the news of George's extra errand, which although annoying, would mean that he could now travel back to London with them.

Foggy declined the proposal, saying that he'd promised his mates that he'd be working the attractions and spending a few days with them.

They finished their food and complimented Al on his culinary delights.

He leaned forward over the counter and handed them each a business card.

"If you get the chance, look my cousin up. He's got a late-night Indian street food wagon, based in Finsbury Park."

Dave looked at the card which read '**Curry Me Home**'.

After assuring Al that they would, they began a leisurely stroll back to the digs.

Chapter 28

Bill And Ben
The Flowerpot Men!

THE SOUND OF an incoming text to Foggy's phone signalled the start of the new day.

It was from Liberty, notifying them she would be with them in twenty minutes.

They all stirred from their sleeping bags and Joe left the room, clutching his wash bag.

After abluting, he returned to pass comment about the lack of activity from the other guests and remarked that a church mouse would be very much at home here!

Once they were all fully upright and clothed, they gathered their belongings, made their way down to the hallway and stood gazing out of the large front window.

They noticed that something resembling a Wild West railroad train hauling some decorative carriages was wending its way along the road in their direction.

Watching it draw closer, it began to slow, and come to a halt directly outside the building.

An energetic figure bounded down from the carriage and bounced up the staircase: it was Liberty who stood on the front porch signalling for them to open the door.

Swinging the large door open allowed her to spring in and embrace each one of them with her customary hug.

She then declared, "Your carriage awaits."

They all descended the stairs and Liberty introduced the driver, who was another trim-looking 'carny' called Ivy.

"Ivy owns this splendid beast and she runs trips along the front and around town."

"Nice wheels," said Dave.

Ivy responded by stating that 'she' was an original 1960s Italian Dotto, exceptionally rare and much sought-after.

"It's the Rolls Royce of land trains.

"I've had offers to buy her from all four corners of the world."

"And from Clint," exclaimed Liberty.

"From all four corners of the world," murmured Joe, with a sarcastic nuance.

Must be what qualifies you for a career in land train business, he thought.

However, his cynical assumption soon backfired when Ivy professed that the train was worth at least £40K.

After lessons had been learned, especially by Joe, Ivy ferried them on board, and even though the whole train was empty, they inexplicably all squashed together in the front seat of the first carriage.

Once settled, Liberty told Foggy that she'd promised Ivy some Acapulco Gold in exchange for their journey.

She obviously wasn't referring to money.

Foggy replied with his thumb.

During the journey, whenever the train came alongside pedestrians a strange phenomenon occurred: it triggered them to make a curious bent-knuckle, aerial-pulling motion.

However, the coinciding whistle poops from the steam trumpet mounted on the top of the loco soon resolved the mystery.

After innumerable accommodating, but very annoying blasts, they finally arrived at the entrance to Liberty's home.

Foggy rooted out one of his trademark small leather pouches and stuffed it with the agreed 'toll payment'.

Liberty took it to the front of the train and with a bro five handclasp she slipped the payment to Ivy.

They disembarked and Ivy clunked the loco into gear in preparation to move on.

As the train wheels rolled forward, Dave, Joe and Foggy all felt compelled to perform the whistle signal, and as the train glided away, Ivy indulged them with several extra-long and loud blasts.

"That was entertaining," said Dave.

"And informative," said Joe reflecting upon his erroneous character assessment.

Passing the 'Privet' sign, they strolled across the grass towards Liberty's caravan.

Ahead of them was a ramshackle group of scruffy-looking individuals who, on spotting Foggy, all began singing the Bill and Ben, Flowerpot Men signature tune.

They then raced over and greeted him with a variety of intricate handshakes, shoulder-bumps and hair-ruffling.

Liberty ignored the commotion and continued walking. Dave and Joe decided to follow her.

After concluding their welcoming rituals, Foggy trotted over to inform Joe and Dave that he would catch up with them in a few days.

After jogging back to the entourage they all disappeared into the fairground.

"He's obviously well-known and liked in these parts," said Joe.

"Yes, they call him 'Little Weed', for obvious reasons, and it's also why they sing the Bill and Ben song."

On approaching Liberty's caravan, she muttered that something was ODD!

"What is?" asked Dave.

"Well, the combo was here this morning," and she drew their attention to the flattened impression of the wheels pressed into the damp grass.

The word Shit pinged around inside Dave's brain like a silver ball in a pinball machine: it'd better not have been nicked!

After closer inspection, Liberty noticed there were tyre tracks leading from the parking spot towards the wooden tower.

They followed the trail to the wooden wall which towered up in front of them. As they stood there, they were confronted by the sound of roaring, popping motorbike engines and rattling wooden planks.

They hurriedly ascended the staircase to reach the viewing platform, and to his horror Dave saw the front wheel of the combo lurch above the top of the wall.

As it moved lower down the wall, Dave could see that it was Clint who was ferociously circumnavigating the wall on George's Combo.

Holy fuck, I'm a dead man, thought Dave.

He grimaced as Clint piloted another half a dozen hair-raising circuits before deciding to ease the throttle and guide the combo back down to base.

"Pretty impressive," said Liberty, oblivious to the reputation of the vehicle's owner and the dire consequences had there been any mishap.

"Dangerous," said Joe, being just as conscious of the gravity of what they'd just witnessed. "I think we need to get those wheels out of there!"

They hastily descended and entered the arena through a tower wall doorway that had been opened. As they entered, they were greeted with the smell of hot engine oil, petrol, loud backfiring sounds, and a beaming Clint.

Clint was extremely animated and claimed that after pressing the combo's booster button the adrenalin rush inspired him to "See what she could do, man. I'd sure like to employ the mother who engineered that," he said.

"I'm not sure if she's a mother, but it was a woman who tuned it," said Joe.

"Whatever, I'd still like them on my team.

"If you fancy selling the combo, then I fancy buying, what d'ya say?"

"I'd say we can't, it's not ours to sell," said Dave, now very eager to get the bike out of the danger zone.

"Shame," said Clint, "she's just the badger," and he took a lustful, lingering look at it before handing over the key. "Ask the owner. I'm sure we could do a deal."

I'm sure you couldn't, thought Dave as he helped Joe manoeuvre the combo outside and wheel it back to Liberty's caravan.

While they checked for damage, Liberty explained that Clint's colloquial 'just the badger' saying meant it was 'exactly what he was looking for'.

"I don't think it is!" said Dave.

Satisfied that no damage was done, they changed into their leathers and thanked Liberty for her hospitality. After a customary hug, Dave said that he **really** hoped they would meet again soon.

He showed Joe the Butlin's discount voucher and suggested breakfast before collecting George's first acquisition.

That was no sooner said than done, and after polishing off the remains of a full English, Joe said he'd like to investigate the resort. So, utilising a crumpled map left on their breakfast table, they set out to explore. After having circumnavigated most of the camp, they decided to follow a shortcut back to the car park.

The route took them past an area of artificial beach, which the map identified as Sandarts Beach, and the magnificent sand sculptures on display more than justified the name

"Are they sand?" asked Joe.

Ducking beneath a metre-high stretch of bunting in order

to find out, Dave delicately scratched at the edge of one of the statues and it crumbled away.

"Sure is," said Dave, now wanting to capture the scene on his phone.

One of the sculptures that was particularly impressive was a marvellous, life-sized interpretation of the 'Jolly Fisherman'.

Dave activated the camera function on his phone and gently moved it sideways, back, and forth to frame the perfect picture.

While he was doing this, he noticed that a scruffy green plastic milk crate, possibly the sculptor's seat, had been left beneath the sculpture's skipping leg.

"That ruins the shot," said Dave, and he asked Joe to join him and remove it while he took the picture.

Joe ducked under the bunting and began to carefully jiggle and slide the box clear. Once it was, Dave pressed the shutter button, capturing a series of images.

Being happy with a review of the results, he gave Joe the OK to tuck it back.

Unfortunately, before Joe could return the crate, disaster struck, and the sculpture began to crumble.

As it began to trickle a little more rapidly, Joe desperately looked around in the hope of spotting something that might help shore up the early stages of a disastrous sandslide.

Unfortunately, all he saw was a sign declaring that the beach was out of bounds, and warning not to cross the bunting barrier until the sand sculpture competition had been judged.

After drawing Dave's attention to the sign, he asked rhetorically, "What is it with you and sand?"

"ME!" exclaimed Dave.

Before the debate could develop, the sound of approaching voices encouraged them to scarper.

Back at the combo, Dave perched on the saddle and input the name and postcode of Aquatillian into his phone, and Joe confessed that his fear of snakes was on a par with that of spiders.

Unfortunately, due to an anomaly with the address, Dave was too pre-occupied to respond.

The only property he could pinpoint on the map was a pub called The Fish and Eels.

After a few more attempts resulting in the same outcome, Dave decided to activate the route button and worry about finding the place when they got there.

The automated voice instructed them to turn right in 150 metres.

Chapter 29

Fish Fingers!

TWENTY-FIVE MINUTES later, they arrived in a sparsely populated area, and the teardrop destination pointer indicated that journey's end was the riverside property located ahead of them.

Checking the map, the red pointer still listed the property as being the Fish and Eels public house, and with the lack of any other buildings in the vicinity, they felt compelled to carry on towards it.

As they got closer, a tatty, damaged pub sign, propped up against a stack of aluminium barrels, confirmed that it had once been the Fish and Eels pub.

A new sign read: '**Aquatillian Purveyors of Exotic Fish & Reptiles**'.

"There's a word that doesn't get used enough," said Joe.

"What, aquatillian?" said Dave, playing devil's advocate.

"Tit!" said Joe, parking beside the sign to run his finger beneath the word 'Purveyors'.

"PURVEYOR: it's a great word, and let's face it, we're all purveyors of something.

"Even your astrologist is a purveyor."

"Yes, of bleeding false hope," said Dave, striding off towards the entrance.

He held the door ajar with his foot and waited for Joe to catch up with him. When he did, they both entered the building.

It was remarkably dark, humid, and dank, and as the odour permeated their nostrils, the intensity of smell made Joe inadvertently yell out, "BLIMEY!"

"You get used to it," said an exuberant, tousled-haired woman, who had a hint of an Antipodean accent and was wearing a brown bush hat. She stepped forward to greet them.

"In fact, one of our employees eats his lunch in here," she said, in testimony of her statement.

Having been 'once bitten' by his derogatory assumptions, Joe was not about to indulge in another, and particularly not in a place where bitten could be the literal consequence.

So, he held out his hand and introduced himself, and it was 'Tas' Badger who returned the greeting.

She turned and shook hands with Dave.

"That's an uncommon name," he commented.

"I was born in Australia, and Tas is short for Tasmin, and Badger comes from...."

"An old Norfolk saying?" asked Dave.

"Not that I'm aware," said Tas, and she continued to explain that it actually came from "a distant relative called Charlotte Badger. She was a Lincolnshire deportee and Australia's first female pirate."

Speaking before he had digested the historical magnitude of Tas's family tree, Dave remarked that, "With a name like Badger, I guess you were destined for a career in wildlife."

Giving a polite, not-heard-that-one-before, acknowledging smile, Tas went on to inform them that she was also a qualified herpetologist, and although similar-sounding, it had absolutely nothing to do with STDs.

Joe piped up and said, "It's the study of reptiles and amphibians."

He was at it again!

"I'm impressed," said Tas. "Not a lot of people would know that."

"Believe me," said Dave, "Joe's not like a lot of people." Joe gave Dave an old-fashioned look.

"So, what brings you to our scaly neck of the woods?" asked Tas.

"We've come to collect some fish for Ge…" Dave was about to say 'George', but he managed to check himself and say geezer.

"We're collecting fish for Diamond Geezer, on eBay."

"Oh yes, the Pygocentrus nattereri. We've only just got those in; they're pretty lively!"

"Where on earth do you get piranha fish from?" asked Joe.

"From here, and South America," replied Tas, and after the matter-of-fact response, she elaborated by asking if either of them knew that piranha had lived in South American waters for over 25 million years.

Bet Joe did, thought Dave, and he was extremely surprised to hear him say that he didn't, and to confess that carnivorous fish were something he knew little about.

Dave merely added that all he knew was that "Piranha hunted in packs and have fearsome teeth."

"Schools, not packs," said Tas.

"Anyhow, you'll have to wait for Andy. He shouldn't be too long; he's setting up the next tortoise race."

"Tortoise racing!" exclaimed Joe. "Is there such a thing?"

"Sure is," said Tas, "Andy started it, and it's become a fundamental part of our business.

"It began as a joke when Andy filmed two tortoises 'racing' along a hand-drawn track and he uploaded it onto YouTube.

"It went viral and led to a national Bookmaker approaching us to run a tote on the next race.

"We got a lucrative contract; they got a unique money-spinning race.

"It's particularly enjoyed by heavy betting far eastern gamblers."

"You don't race a black one?" asked Joe, beaming at Dave.

"They don't exist," replied Tas, not realising that it was an 'in joke' and rhetorical question.

Then just like Joe, Tas imparted her knowledge about black tortoises.

"They're one of the four mythical symbols in the Chinese constellation, signifying longevity and wisdom, but they look more like a turtle than a tortoise."

Joe turned to Dave to comment that if it had been a **tortoise** and not **Pluto** in Uranus, things might have turned out differently.

Tas looked totally bewildered.

"Excuse my friend," said Dave, "he's a trainee clown."

Thankfully for Tas, Andy entered the room.

He was tall and reedy, and he displayed an array of weathered tattoos. He wore camouflage clothing and a bush tucker's hat.

Tas spoke to say that "These guys have come to collect the Diamond Geezer's fish," and after formal introductions, Andy asked them if they'd come far.

"London," replied Joe.

"That's not a bad a journey, especially if you're in an SUV. What wheels you got?"

"A motorcycle combi," blurted Joe, almost wanting to hysterically laugh out loud at the ridiculousness of what he'd just said.

If there was ever an unsuitable vehicle in which to collect piranhas with, then that was it, AND they'd left the protective top behind.

Seeing the tanks of wild reptiles suddenly brought home the further realisation of their stupidity.

It appeared as if River had intentionally set them up with the combi as payback for Foggy's jibe.

"I'm sure it'll do the job," said Andy in a half-heartedly reassuring manner.

"What have you brought to put the fish in?"

Joe was now totally stranded between laughter and tears, and he just couldn't bring himself to say the sidecar.

So, he answered the only way possible, by saying he thought that they were going to be packed.

Andy replied by saying that, as a rule of thumb and due to their hazardous nature, he would usually deliver this type of fish in his specially converted van, especially the ones that they were about to collect.

"These are red-bellied piranha which have the worst reputation for aggressive behaviour," he elaborated by saying that "the perception that piranhas only ate the dead and dying" was a "total myth".

He then held up his left hand and displayed three missing fingertips as proof.

"These are real fish fingers!" he said.

"However, your friend Diamond Geezer insisted on collection, so before you leave, you'll have to sign an indemnity form.

"Before that, I'll need to look at your transport and work out the best way to load the fish safely."

They all traipsed outside, and Andy to his credit, on seeing the combo, retained his composure.

Joe, on the other hand, really, really, wanted to cry!

Andy said, "It's an interesting one," thoughtfully resting his chin on his knuckles.

He asked Tas to get him a measuring tape.

On her return they set about measuring the compartment of the sidecar.

The conclusion reached was that it was too small for a vivarium terrarium or any suitably-sized fish tank, and it was too narrow for a water butt.

He removed his hat and he scratched the top of his head.

Dave was as reticent as Joe to mention the fact that the sidecar was lined and suggest that they could fill it water.

However, the task had to be completed so he mentioned it.

Andy raised his eyebrows and said, "Well, as there's no seat, and lacking any other viable solution, that could work."

"What a relief!"

"The only thing we'd need to ensure is to seal the open-top, as splashing tends to make piranhas more belligerent. The last thing that you want near your body parts are eight agitated, predatory fish!

"Polythene would have done the trick but we're clean out.

"We used the last roll of it yesterday, and we won't be getting a delivery till late tomorrow."

"What about Edmund's Hardware?" said Tas.

"They're out," replied Andy. "I tried to get some from them yesterday, and I think they're on the same delivery as us."

Dave, anxious to fulfil the WIIFU, threw caution and common sense to the wind and asked, "What about cling film?"

"It could work," said Andy.

"Could it?" asked Dave, in straw-clutching desperation.

"Would it be strong enough?"

"I think so," said a now more optimistic Andy, "if you purchased enough to wrap around the body at least a dozen times it should do the job."

"Where's Edmund's?" asked Joe.

"It's about a mile further on," replied Tas, pointing out the direction.

"You'll see a disused red telephone box on the left and Edmund's is about a quarter of a mile away on the right."

"Come on, Dave," said Joe, firing up the bike.

"Back shortly," exclaimed Dave, plonking his backside on the pillion seat.

After about three-quarters of a mile, the red telephone box did appear on the left-hand side of the road and the hardware store, as predicted, was just a little further on.

The remains of original Michelin tyre and Exide battery signs, plus the two globe-topped fuel pumps, indicated that Edmund's was housed inside an old converted garage workshop.

The top of the property was now clearly living accommodation and the ground floor had been remodelled into a Dickensian-styled shop front.

There were two enormous original wooden entrance doors at each side of the shop windows which when shut would enclose and secure the entire retail frontage.

The two old-fashioned globe-topped pumps displayed the name '**Edmund's Hardware Emporium**'.

Pulling into the forecourt, Joe dismounted and headed straight towards the petrol pumps, and after pointing out the word 'Emporium', he was disappointed to discover that they were only fibreglass replicas, used purely to advertise the store.

As Dave caught up, Joe asked him just how pissed off would he be to come across these on a dark, rainy, low-on-fuel night?

"Extremely," said Dave, opening the shop door for Joe to enter first.

Inside there was not a centimetre of wasted sales space.

It was crammed to the rafters with gadgets, gizmos and supplies for the home and garden. The walls cascaded with every item imaginable.

It was a feast for the eyes and was indeed a store that deserved to be called an emporium.

A middle-aged man wearing a brown cotton storeman's coat appeared from behind a laden glass haberdasher's cabinet.

A name tag on his lapel identified him as 'Evan'.

"Good morning, gentleman. If you need help to find something specific, just let me know."

"I don't think I've ever seen such a variety of goods," said Dave in bewilderment.

"We sell anything from toothpicks to telegraph poles, our motto is, if Edmund's doesn't have it – then, it doesn't exist!"

He then pointed to a large enamel wall sign that conveyed the same message.

"I can believe that," said Dave.

"Except for fuel," said Joe, still rankled about the fake petrol pumps.

"Well, we do have an emergency supply of petrol and diesel in the old garage storage tanks behind the store.

"We also sell paraffin, butane, logs, and coal.

"So, what are you looking for?"

To be asking for clingfilm was causing Joe to experience the same uncomfortable embarrassment he'd felt in telling Andy about the combi.

Fortunately, this didn't affect Dave in the same way, and he readily chirped up, "Clingfilm.

"The widest and strongest you have please."

This store owner didn't bat an eyelid, he simply asked, "How many?"

"Six," said Joe, "and a couple of rolls of gaffer tape."

After climbing the three wooden steps that led into another stockroom, Evan temporarily vanished from sight.

Moments later he returned with the goods.

"There you are, that's cleaned us out," he said, stacking them onto the top of his glass counter. "That should keep your food fresh."

Or us from being fresh food, thought Joe.

After paying, they bid farewell and headed back to Aquatillian to load the fish.

Arriving back, Tas told them to drive the combo to the rear of the property where Andy was waiting to load the fish.

Behind the property were a variety of stock pools and tanks and Andy was lifting an industrial hosepipe from a little green Gator truck.

As Joe cut the engine, Andy informed them that the hose

was ex-Fire Brigade and that he'd bought it for twenty-five quid on eBay.

After he had unrolled the pipe, he coupled it to his private water hydrant.

"This cost enough to install," he said, screwing the connectors together.

Once done, he placed the hose into the sidecar and said, "'The moment of truth', let's see if she leaks."

He strode back and twisted a long brass 'key', and the water rapidly gushed through the pipe, quickly filling the compartment.

Fortunately, it did not leak.

"I'm impressed," said Andy and as the water reached the desired level, he shut it off.

"Now comes the exciting part," he said, pulling on some heavy-duty leather gloves.

He asked Joe to roll the bike slightly closer to the holding pond, and he retrieved a sturdy, metal-handled mesh fishnet from his wagon.

Slowly he individually scooped the fish from the pond and gently lowered them into the sidecar, and as intimated, they were incredibly lively!

After all eight had been transferred, he stuffed the net back onto the truck and said, "We'd better wrap the critters."

"Got the Clingfilm?"

Dave opened the Edmund's paper carrier bag and handed Andy the Clingfilm.

They watched in relief as Andy used five rolls to circumnavigate and seal the top of the sidecar.

"We bought some gaffer tape, just to be safe," said Joe, handing it to Andy.

Andy obliged and used a roll and a half to cover the Clingfilm.

"Job's a good 'n," said Andy. "Unfortunately, I can't punch

any air holes into it because it has to be watertight, so you'll need to get them unloaded in the next four hours, max.

"All we need to do now is to get your scrawl on the paperwork and that's it."

They all returned into the store, where Tas was placing a snake inside the purchaser's customised wooden crate.

Andy made his way behind the long counter and began to tap the keys on his laptop, and Dave stood opposite him.

Joe distanced himself to the furthest end of the counter to keep some space between him and the wriggling reptile.

Andy looked at Joe and then Dave, who explained snake phobia.

"It's called ophidiophobia," said Andy.

"I'm sure he knows that," said Dave.

Andy finished typing and printed out several sheets of A4 printed paper.

Andy checked them and made up two sets of paperwork. He placed them side by side on the countertop and turned them to face Dave.

Using his pen, Andy ran the tip of it along the wording to highlight the essential points.

He stopped at the wording, 'Agreement between Aquatillian' and said, "US," then carried along to the name 'DIAMOND GEEZER' and said, "YOU!"

He continued with the pointer and read out the critical bold wording.

I, the undersigned, confirm that it is my decision to undertake the transport of eight red-bellied piranha fish (Pygocentrus nattereri), purchased from Aquatillian.

It is agreed that upon leaving their curtilage, Aquatillian will have no further responsibility for the transport, unloading or the storage of the piranha fish.

FULL legal obligation for this transfer to Diamond Geezer and his transport personnel.

The purchaser and the nominated signatories agree to be lawfully obligated to indemnify Aquatillian against any claims brought through accidental or deliberate negligence or mishap.

"That's the important bit," said Andy, "but you should also read the safety information before you sign."

WARNING

PIRANHA FISH ARE DANGEROUS!

To avoid accidents, it is of the utmost importance that you always respect these fish!

Respect the power of the piranha, its razor-sharp teeth, and its ability to perform lightning-fast strikes.

Respect the fish's nervous disposition and personal space.

They WILL attack if frightened.

NEVER dangle your fingers or toes in water populated by Piranhas.

I, the undersigned, have read, fully understood, and agree to be legally bound by this document.

Dave and Andy signed both copies, and the documents were then witnessed by Tasmin Badger.

As they bid their adieus, Tas handed them both a FREE Aquatillian decal, and they headed off to collect George's extra purchase.

Chapter 30

Spuffle, Squit And Higgle!

A SLOW, STEADY journey and cautious navigation of a long, narrow, potholed driveway leading up to the address given by River added an extra 40 minutes to their originally predicted ETA.

At the end of the driveway was a small cluster of tumble-down buildings and a shabby farmhouse, all of which were in the same state of neglect and disrepair as the driveway.

The crunching shingle in the courtyard announced their arrival and instigated the opening of the farmhouse door by an elderly, rustic countrywoman wearing a floppy hat and a T-shirt that was stretched out of shape by her unfettered bosom.

A faded printed logo that read 'NARC' adorned the crumpled top, and, considering who she was dealing with, made this outrageously funny.

It later transpired that NARC was an acronym for Norma's Animal Rescue Centre.

Speaking in a voice that indicated that she hadn't moved too far from home in her lifetime, she said, "Weren't zackly sure wat time yew'd be 'ere, so I was just 'avn me wittales.

"I'd put Betsy on if I'd knewn."

She then asked why 'thur sidecar' was wrapped in film; "It looks 'ceptionally duzzy to me."

"It's duzzy alright," said Dave, curtailing the conversation.

Norma then asked if they'd come for Pia.

"If Pia's Italian, green and looks like an oversized wheelbarrow, then madam, we have indeed come for Pia," said Joe, engaging the peculiar pantomime dame's voice that he'd used to answer his phone last night.

"Weird!"

The old woman was as baffled as Dave was and asked,

"Do 'e alwys spuffle a loada ol' squit?"

Dave was once again confused by 'nutty badger' country dialect.

So instead of a replying in words, he opened his phone, scrolled to the image that River had sent him, and 'shewed' it to the old woman.

The old lady, Norma, peered at it, and commented, "Thass Mia, come alonga me."

She turned and strode briskly across the courtyard to one of the heavily timbered buildings. Joe and Dave followed her.

Standing in front of pair of tall gable doors, she stooped to pick up a brick, which she then used to clobber the solid oak latch that was holding them together.

She proceeded to forcefully drag each door open, revealing a vast medieval timbered framed interior and the minuscule green truck.

Before venturing inside, Norma commented, "Me an my cuzn hed a roight ol barney. He said that yer boss wern't our sort – an that we shunt hev any truck wi' him! – but cos 'e didn' higgle, I let 'im 'av 'er."

In presumption that all villainous types would be versed in the art of 'higgling' (whatever it was), Dave pondered why George hadn't higgled.

As they stepped inside the barn and moved closer to Pia, the numberplate offered a possible solution to that conundrum.

It read '**AR53HOL**' and, guessing that the plates were potentially worth more than the asking price of the vehicle, it could explain why George hadn't higgled.

"Yer boss also 'greed yew'll do a delivery for me."

She pointed a crooked finger towards what looked like an oversized packing crate tucked into the corner of the barn.

As they walked towards it, a series of sizeable holes drilled around the sides and into the top of the box became visible.

On getting significantly closer, the box shuddered, confirming that it was housing a live occupant.

It resembled the box that Tas was loading at Aquatillian, so Joe asked if it was a snake and stepped sharply backwards, just in case.

"No, but judging by yer fizzog, yew could be this chap's uncle!

"Yew know what it is, don't yew?"

And as if the scenario wasn't puzzling enough, they were now being asked to solve a bumpkin riddle.

"His uncle?" enquired Dave pointing at the crate.

"Yeah, his uncle," said the Norfolk dumpling, seamlessly sliding a banana from her pocket through one of the larger holes and into the crate.

"It's a monkey," said a very relieved Joe.

"Teknically speakin', it's not a monkey," said Norma, "'e's not fully grown, so 'e's still only a chimp."

Now that the box housed a seemingly playful primate, they were more confident in venturing closer to it.

"P'leece confiscated 'e from a shyster shewman, thay fetch 'im 'ere.

"'E needs to git oover to Gus's place in Newmarket, 'e'll 'av a good 'om there."

With the use of some old scaffold boards and a lot of effort, they managed eventually to slide the crate onto the truck.

Unlike the document produced by Aquatillian, the only

thing to sign here was, literally, the back of a crumpled fag packet, which simply said, "I collected a green van."

They did a final check of the cargo, and after Norma told them to keep 'yew a troshin', they set off in a two-vehicle convoy towards the Zookeeper's house to deliver the fish.

After several miles, Joe, who had been driving at a pace that respected his hazardous cargo, suddenly swerved sharply right then back left again.

The manoeuvre was so quick it created the impression that he'd inadvertently touched the booster button.

Following closely behind, Dave suddenly and unexpectedly hit something in the road which launched 'Pia' into the air.

Although startling, it explained the reason for Joe swerving.

As it thumped back onto the road the back panels of the truck clattered, and the elastic bungee straps holding the crate secure pinged off and into obscurity, and the monkey let out an ear-piercing, "Ooh ooh eee eee aah aah!"

Apart from the loss of bungee straps, Dave seemed to have had got away without inflicting more serious damage – thank God!

Explaining anything more extreme to River, or George, was not an accomplishment that was on his bucket list.

As he proceeded onwards, he squinted into the side mirror to see if he could identify what it was that he'd just driven over, but apart from it being quite sizeable and dirty brownish in colour, he couldn't make out what it was.

He shrugged his shoulders and carried on going, as did the chattering monkey in the crate.

Eventually they arrived at the Zookeeper's property and they drove into the grounds, and up to a sizeable swimming pool where they had been instructed to unload the fish.

Dave stopped and parked slightly back from the edge, and Joe cautiously manoeuvred the combo closer to the water's edge.

Dave decamped from the van, and after a quick visual check revealed no damage, he joined Joe at the poolside.

"You decided to hit that lump in the road, then?" Joe asked mockingly.

"Of course, I did!" said Dave, snapping at the bait. "Who wouldn't?"

"Opportunities to destroy a criminal nutjob's new toy, invalidate an underworld agreement, AND get a 'duck chipper' onto your case don't come along every day!"

"So, when they do, you've got to take them – pillock."

"That's a relief," said Joe. "I was worried you hadn't seen it."

Having got that off his chest, Dave lowered himself onto the ground to assess the fish deployment situation, and after careful evaluation he said he thought that the angle of the bike was all wrong.

With the nose cone in its current position, he believed that majority of the fish would probably miss the water and be left flailing about outside the pool.

He felt it might be more feasible and sensible if they moved the combo further along.

Joe agreed and decided to move it to the midway point of the pool.

He restarted the bike, which for some inexplicable reason, noisily backfired.

The sound alarmed the monkey in the crate and in sheer panic, it battered the loosened lid clean off and sprung out.

With an almighty leap, it jumped onto the cab roof, bounced onto the handlebars of the bike and instantly rebounded onto Joe's head, which it used as a springboard to leap up and onto the platform at the top of the waterslide.

During the brief interaction with the motorbike handlebars, one of the primate's hairy digits must have touched the booster button, causing the combo to launch forward and into the pool.

Another consequence of this episode was that the blue

gobstopper release knob struck Dave's leg, causing the nose cone to open.

The only upside to this disastrous situation was that by using Joe's head as a springboard, the chimp had knocked him clear of any harm's way.

It had also saved him from following the bike into the water.

KUSHTI BOK!

As they haplessly watched the bike burbling and slowly sinking deeper, their concern was temporarily eased by a laughter spurt when Joe commented, "For Gawd's sawk, 'e's a bloomn barmy barstard, an – thass a fact!"

His attempt to mimic the old lady's Norfolk accent had resulted in it sounding more like Dick Van Dyke's entertaining rendition of cockney Bert in Mary Poppins.

Their manic laughter was short-lived, and it dissipated as quickly as it had emerged.

They watched in silent disbelief as the final part of the combo glugged and slid beneath the surface.

"It would be in the bloody deep end," said Joe, not knowing what else to say.

As they watched, a blue oily swirl floated up and created an amazing marbling effect on the surface

However, the result was momentary, as a tribe of frenzied fish gnawed their way to the surface and created havoc with the pattern.

Joe sheepishly announced that, albeit this was an absurd travesty, they had actually disposed of the wheels.

Dave replied saying, "As it was in neither a discreet or permanent manner, I'm not sure if River or George would agree with that!"

"Well whatever, we HAVE TO retrieve the number plate," said Joe, "if we can get it back to River, perhaps we needn't mention this little hiccup."

"And just how the fuck do you suggest we rescue the plate

from a piranha-infested pool?" asked Dave, semi-rhetorically and undoubtedly now in a panic.

"Well," said Joe, "clearly, one of us will have to go in and get it!"

"Clearly, it won't be me," said Dave adamantly. "I once watched a film of a bloke throwing a huge chunk of meat into the Amazon and within moments piranha fish appeared and savaged it to the bone.

"So, bollocks to getting in there, but if you think it's an option, knock yourself out!"

"I'm only imagining that the repercussions of returning without the plate," said Joe, "might be just as dangerous."

"You want to know what I think?" said Dave.

"I think the one who created this friggin' mess should be the one to sort it out," and pointing to the top of the water slide, he yelled, "We should make the poxy monkey go in and get it!"

"I don't think that's going to happen," said Joe, and he reiterated the need to stay calm and think logically.

"If we had something to keep the fish occupied at one end of the pool, it could buy some time to dip in and retrieve the plate."

"Yeah, I already told you, throw the fucking monkey in," said Dave, looking up at the yawning scratching primate.

"I was thinking more along the lines of going back to retrieve the roadkill that you skilfully hotdogged, we could use it as bait."

THAT, Dave had to admit, was not a bad idea and it could just work and, although it still left the issue of who would be entering the water unresolved, it was a plan.

On returning with a dead badger stuffed inside the crate, they were perturbed to see an army of uniformed people all frantically scurrying about the Zookeeper's grounds.

At first sight they resembled the police, but the blue logos emblazoned on the front of their outfits and the parked vehicles in the grounds indicated that they were from the RSPCA.

After discreetly parking just beyond the entrance, they acted as concerned citizens and boldly strolled through the gates towards one of the inspectors.

"All right, mate – oh sorry, luv," said Joe, realising it was a cropped-haired woman that he'd addressed, "is there a problem here? Can we help?"

"Not really," said the woman. "Someone's called us because they said they saw an ape bounding about in the grounds."

"Really – have you spotted one or do you think it's a hoax?" asked Dave, trying hard not to show that he already knew that it wasn't a hoax.

"Nothing's been seen yet, but we have discovered a shoal of piranha and a motorcycle in the swimming pool.

"It looks suspicious, so we've called the police."

Fuck, shit, bollocks, thought Dave, now REALLY concerned for their wellbeing.

In his moment of sheer dread, he became unaware that Joe had ambled over to the poolside.

Returning from his sortie Joe took hold of Dave's forearm and gently but firmly spun him round to face the entrance.

He then proceeded to usher Dave towards it.

Along the way, the officer they had spoken to was inspecting a large tree, and Joe stopped and called over: "Not much we can do here, so we'll leave you to it."

The woman raised an open hand and waved them goodbye and Joe reciprocated the gesture.

As they strode purposefully back towards 'pia', Dave asked "what about the number plate?

Joe dipped his hand into his jacket pocket and revealed the top of a soggy piece of plastic.

"It's not –?" said Dave.

"It is," said Joe, stuffing it back.

Once safely ensconced back inside the minuscule cab Dave turned to Joe and asked, "HOW?"

"Don't know, it was just floating on the surface. Perhaps the three badgers brought us luck!"

"KUSHTI fucking BOK," said Dave. As he exhaled, and the tension visibly drained from his shoulders, an equally relieved Joe said, "It's time to get this baby back to its crèche."

Dave gave a push on the accelerator and they were heading for 'home'.

After a trouble-free journey, they made it back to the garage in high spirits.

They had accomplished George's missions and the finances would now be forthcoming and everything could return to normal.

As they drove into the yard, the shuttered door of the garage opened and out stepped River, accompanied by a man wearing his baseball cap backwards.

River indicated that they should park opposite the doorway, and she walked over to a parked Jaguar.

She opened the driver's door, popped the latch, and then propped up the bonnet.

She crouched over the engine and engaged in a lengthy discussion with cap man.

After a while they emerged, and River snapped the bonnet shut, shook hands, and then strode decisively back into their direction.

"Nice…" she said, admiring the tiny truck, "…very nice!

"And the crate?" she asked.

Thinking on his feet and deliberately neglecting to mention the content, Dave answered that it was something that George had arranged.

Satisfied with the answer, River turned her attention to the fact that only Dave and Joe had returned with the vehicle and, obviously still pissed at Foggy, she asked where 'Knobhead' was?

Dave felt slightly guilty that by responding to the enquiry that he was in some way endorsing River's character assassination. However, it was more important to get the task completed, and cash in the WIIFU.

So he replied, "Foggy's staying up in Skeggy for a while."

"That's not surprising," she said. "I'd heard that Skegness was famous for its winkles!"

Dave and Joe got out from the vehicle and handed River the key, the paperwork and the magnetic numberplate.

She turned and they followed her back into the workshop.

River pointed to a large, crudely-constructed wooden board that was covered in brass hooks containing numerous car keys.

After some darting eye movements, Dave eventually spotted his key, and removed it.

He then awkwardly asked River if she knew when he might expect to get paid out on the WIIFU?

She said that Greg had the answer to that, and "He'll tell you over a healthy yoghurt and blueberry breakfast at **'Crêpe Expectations'**.

"He wants you to meet him there at 8 tomorrow morning."

Rummaging through a well-thumbed collection of flyers that were piled on her desk, River located and handed them one for **'Crêpe Expectations'**.

As they left the building, they hoped that their work there was well and truly done!

Chapter 31

Crêpe Un-Expectations

DAVE, AND THANKFULLY Joe, both met as agreed, at Crêpe Expectations at 7.45am. They decided it was prudent to wait for Greg to join them before ordering.

At precisely 7.59am the Bistro door swung open and Greg breezed, in carrying a large black pilot's briefcase.

Spotting Dave in the corner, he made his way over to the booth and sat on the bench seat opposite them.

He pushed his case along the seat. Dave introduced Joe and, after shaking hands, Greg grabbed a menu and proceeded to flick it open.

He said that he could highly recommend the yoghurt and blueberry crêpe and any of the milkshakes.

"But you guys have what you want, it's all Kushti!"

Not wishing to invoke any type of Kushti, especially by disagreeing with Greg's recommendation, they both nodded and muttered acceptance of his choice.

Greg turned and raised a finger in the air.

A beret-wearing waitress, dressed provocatively in French maid outfit, responded by shimmying over to their table. She told them her name was Safran.

Sadly (as it had with Clint), the estuary accent immediately diluted the whole French café feel.

Greg ordered for them all, which hopefully indicated that he would also be picking up the tab.

He watched Safran meander away from the table and disappear behind the counter; he then returned his gaze back to Dave and Joe.

"I understand the job was not entirely a good'n," he said enquiringly.

Dave felt that, as this had been his quest, it should be he who answered the criticism.

"Well, in fairness, I wouldn't say it was a bad'n."

He continued to parry confidently by saying, "We did achieve all we were asked to!"

Not being exactly sure as to how Greg was going to react to Dave's potentially flippant and challenging reply, Joe slid backwards into his seat.

"Well I don't recall anyone asking you to dump the combo into a swimming pool, lose a 120lb ape, and bring a dead badger back, do you?" asked Greg.

"I accept that we had a few hiccups and had to improvise, but I still don't think we did a bad job!"

The words "Stop poking the bear!" were screaming inside Joe's head, and as if she had a mystical sixth sense and could hear Joe's mental plea, Safran appeared at the table with their drinks, and all-out war was avoided!

In anticipation of the imminent arrival of their food, Greg tucked his napkin under his chin and into the neck of his shirt.

He opened his briefcase and removed his phone.

He tapped the screen several times and propped it up against the condiments holder so that they could all clearly see it.

"It's not up to me to decide if the job was a good'n or not," said Greg, "it's up to George, he's the boss."

As he said that, the screen flickered, and George's foreboding face appeared on screen.

He looked pensive and launched into a tirade of criticism.

"Yours is the second WIIFU cock-up that I've had THIS WEEK!

"Even though it's not such a disaster as the scarpered Rasta's burger fail, I'm still not happy!

"When word reached me about, the combo, an ape, and a dead badger, I thought, if I'd wanted clowns to do my work, I could have gone to the circus to hire them!

"I don't give a rat's arse about King Louie returning to the wild or having to dispose of a maggot-ridden badger carcass.

"MY displeasure is because instead of gassing the swan, you bleedin' drowned it, and after the fish were removed from the pool the Zookeeper had to find another way to dispose of their food."

He momentarily turned away from the screen and mumbled something to someone lurking in the background.

After a brief exchange of words his face refilled the screen.

"I understand you retrieved the numberplate and did get the truck back to the garage in one piece so, I suppose we must be grateful for small mercies.

"However, I'm still not impressed, you've still let me down!

"In my book a deal is a deal, and half a job warrants half the pay!

"So, I'm withholding 50% of the WIIFU."

He moved his face much closer and peered straight into the screen and raised a challenging eyebrow.

"However, I'm not an unfair or an unreasonable man, and I know that you need the cabbage, so I'm prepared to give you another chance.

"If you agree to undertake another mission for me, I'll overlook your little mishaps and on successful, SUCCESSFUL completion, Greg will transfer the remaining half of the funds to your account.

"I think that's fair and reasonable, don't you?"

He pulled back from the screen and awaited a response.

Dave believed that he'd already done an extra 50% work by

collecting the truck, and it now seemed that he'd also fulfilled the burger WIIFU. So, he'd done enough to warrant payment for two and a half WIIFUs. Therefore George's interpretation of being fair and reasonable was none too accurate.

However, seeing George's great big threatening phizog staring out at him from the phone, Dave wasn't going to tell him that or argue his point.

He didn't want to end up with both George and Humph on his case, and asking for details of the assignment before agreeing to do it would be another risky gambit.

He really needed the full payment, but it was obvious that without agreement he could jeopardise the half payment already promised.

Before Dave could respond, George's face was replaced on the screen by a set of extremely large knuckles, and a stern voice called out the word, "DEAL?"

After a slight hesitancy, Dave jabbed forward a clenched fist and reciprocated the gesture by interactively bumping his knuckles against George's electronically, sealing his agreement.

"A wise decision," said George. "I'll be in touch."

By this time Greg had devoured his breakfast and drunk his milkshake. he ended the call and placed the phone back in his heavy-duty briefcase.

He removed his napkin, put it on his empty plate, stood up and said, "I'll sort the first payment into your account.

"You'll be hearing from me again soon!

"By the way, I eat here a lot now, so be sure you leave Safran a good tip when you settle the bill." He then turned and left.

Dave and Joe had hardly begun to eat their meals and they looked at each other in utter amazement, both of George's proclamations and of Greg leaving them with the bill.

Feeling slightly awkward that they were both sitting side by side, Dave pushed Greg's plate to the end of the table and moved himself and his breakfast opposite Joe.

"How did that happen?" said Joe in reference to being saddled with the bill.

"Don't know," said Dave, "I'm more concerned about the burger WIIFU cock-up. That must have been the Lenny extra special – George will kill us if he finds out what happened!"

"I REALLY wouldn't worry about that," said Joe. "Sadly the ''ungry man' has sealed his own fate. If George does catch up with him, he's not going to believe a word he says!"

"You're totally right," said Dave and they both sat and ate in partially relieved silence.

Safran again glided over to their table, and after removing Greg's plate, she held out an oversized scratch card depicting some French-themed graphics.

"It's our new promotion.

"I forgot to bring it with your order.

"You get a chance of winning a trip to Paris, a crêpe recipe book, a free meal and several other prizes listed on the back."

Joe took the card and twisted it over to read the back.

He then fruitlessly fumbled his pockets before asking Dave if he had a coin.

Dave leaned sideways to raise his rump and slide his hand into his back pocket and withdrew his Thunderbirds leather wallet.

On seeing it Joe raised his eyebrows and Dave responded to the unspoken enquiry with the words… "Ask my mother!"

He parted the sides of the wallet and unzipped the coin compartment.

As he poked around, a mangled dog-eared piece of card flipped out and onto the table.

He stopped fumbling inside his wallet to see what it was.

After uncurling and flattening the unsubstantial piece of cardboard, he turned it around, over, and then around again, to reveal that it was in fact a battered but still intact scratch card.

He handed it to Joe, saying, "It was the one that the old hag at the bus stop didn't get."

"Look at the name on it," said Joe, moving it closer to Dave's face.

Dave held Joe's wrist to re-focus his eyes to read the wording.

Black Cat Jackpot – reveal THREE black cats to win!

Dave returned to rummaging in his wallet, fished out the silver Manx crown that he'd found on the train and handed it to Joe.

"Try that."

Taking hold of it, Joe examined both sides of the coin and asked, "Why would you keep a Manx crown in your wallet?"

"For luck?"

Re-examining it in a bit more detail, Joe said that "Some of these old coins are worth money.

"I knew a bloke who emptied parking meters and he told me that some of the dud coins that people inserted were worth hundreds of pounds. Ironic, really; you should check it out!"

Flattening the Black Cat scratch card, he asked if he should do the honours.

"Might as well," said Dave.

Joe began to scratch away at the symbols and he steadily worked his way across the first row of three.

As he removed the first paw print, it revealed a rabbit's foot, the second a horseshoe and the third a chimney sweep.

Next, he decided to erase the two left-hand vertical symbols and they revealed a BLACK CAT and a horseshoe.

He then scratched away at two of the four remaining symbols and they revealed a rabbit's foot and a chimney sweep.

Tentatively, he hovered the coin above the remaining two panels.

First to show was… a BLACK CAT – he said, "We're on a roll," and held the card aloft to show Dave.

"Don't get your hopes up," said Dave, moving his head nearer, "it's fixed!"

Placing the card back onto the table, Joe cautiously scratched at the last paw print. He looked at it, went quiet and then handed the card over for Dave to check.

"Bloody hell, it's – THREE BLACK CATS.

It really is THREE black cats!"

"Check the prize. What is it?" said a now overly-excited Joe.

Turning the card over, Dave used his index finger to find the answer…

"It's eight and a half grand – eight and a half bloody grand!"

"What about the lucky shooting star double bonus box?" said Joe, exuberantly grabbing the card back.

"Go on Joe, let the silver cat do its black magic."

"One more time, kitty," said Joe, kissing the lucky coin.

He again rubbed the coin delicately over the lucky star symbol.

Flicking away the bulk of the silver rubbings he blew the remainder off and lifted it closer to his face.

"She's done it again," he said, showing Dave the uncovered star.

Dave snatched back the card, checked it, and checked it again. He then raised both arms in the air and started to do a seated cockney jig.

After a few high-fives and Cheshire cat-like grins, Dave realised that, apart from the scratch card win, he also had the funds from half a WIIFU, the tabletop sale and the burger heist.

He was now able to give Humph and his mates their un-won winnings, treat his mum, Joe and Foggy, and…buy a BMW.

To add to his good fortune, Dave also noticed that there was an iconic French *'Steinlen du Chat Noir'* poster hanging on the wall, and he thought to himself: *She was right all along, bloody Madam Patiala was right!*

Pluto really was in Uranus and a black cat did, eventually, transform my finances.

He stood and proclaimed that this called for a celebration, and, in the absence of champagne, suggested raising their crêpes to toast Madam Patiala.

He also stated that "George could poke his poxy WIIFU!"

Joe interceded, "Whilst not wishing to rain on your parade, you know that, according to 'Lord Elpus' and 'The book of George', a fist bump is as good as a signed contract even if it is via the internet.

"So, whether you need his money or not, you've committed to undertake his next task."

Dave lowered the crêpe and momentarily stood in ponderous thought. He then raised the crêpe again, declaring:

"We'll cross that bridge later... Till then, let's just enjoy this very posh **PANCAKE**!"